A Book
of Merlin

A Book
of Merlin

Table of Contents

Merlin's Youth

First Part

1

A lad I was, dark-haired and dark of eye,
    Ever the first to court a danger shown,
    Ever the last to lay my courage down
In face of man or sprite. Strife then ran high
  Betwixt us and the strangers; and the land
  Stirred with a thrill it could not understand.

For 'twas the tie that bound mother and child,
    And strangers would possess her bosom bare,
    And strangers batten on our woodland air,
And strangers trample on our mountains wild;
  And so the earth stirred in stern motherhood,
  And all her children knew in their blood.

Slight-limbed was I, nor challenged feats of strength:
    My great-thewed cousins hurled the massy rock,
    And flung the fir-tree that ten winters' shock
Had left unharmed. Thick shoulders, thighs of length,
  Flat hips, stout buttocks; — they could throw a steer,
  Or drink their shallow wits away the livelong year.

2

Yberha was her name. Across the flood,
Where then a mounded tower in stoutness stood,
    There lived her father; — silent, moody man,
  Caring not who was kind nor who was proud,
  Nor what more than aught else men cried aloud,
    Nor where his neighbour's power stretched its span.

One moonlight night I swam the tide across,
Met the great wave in the middle, saw it toss,
   Tossed a long bowshot in its boiling surge,
  Fought till the flood could know its master there,
  Swam, bold, to the further bank, for earth and air,
   And saw her standing silent on the verge.

The moon played on her head, and yellow hair
Flowed to her waist with never let or care;
   White dress, white arms, shone in the mystic light,
  Pale cheeks, and lips compressed, were desolate:
  She seemed a spirit wandered forth by fate,
   To give a pallid soul to the dead night.

3

She looked toward the moon; and, stooping down,
   Reached backward without gazing, from the sward
   Plucking three strange leaves, and with a careful ward
Knotted them fast enfolded in her gown;
  Nor ever looked but straitly at the moon,
  And murmured weary words to strange sad tune: —

   "Listen maid, listen man,
   Catch bubble who catch can,
   Surge tide, river glide;
   Merge bush, shiver rush:
  Watch, fair lady of the skies!
  Look me, look me in the eyes;
  You shall not see me pick your prize."

I knew not if she were of fairy birth,
   But knew that she was fair, as never yet
   Has man known and been able to forget.
I knew not were she slight or honest worth;
  But knew that how so e'er I lived on earth,

A Book of Merlin

For how so many years, without her it was dearth.

And stepping forth beside her on the dew,
   I said, "The night is lonely in this place,
   The moon is poor protection for your grace;
The wolves are fierce, and those that dare them few:
   Till you find safer guardian I will stand
   Beside you; strong or weak, to your command."

4

And so I turned, proud of my youth and might,
Of skill and courage — for, whate'er the fight,
   The swift eye and the swiftly-reasoning brain,
   Knowing when best to give, and when to take,
   And vantage out of direst chance to make,
   Laughs at the strength that rives an oak in twain; —

Proud of my power, shamed of my nakedness;
Nor caring what this maid with golden tress
   Thought of my sudden speech. For she was mine,
   I cared not how so great her pride or power,
   Nor did her lips smile or her forehead lower,
   Or tears or fire beneath her eyelids shine.

Proud of my power, I knew her ever mine,
Willing or unwilling; so the sun should shine
   The morrow, or the winter bring us snow.
   Strength must bow down to greater strength; and none,
   My proud youth told me, breathed our Western sun
   Woman or man, my subtle force could know.

5

Turned she, a-rustle in the dewy grass: —
   "Strange things, methinks, are come abroad to-night,

When a poor stripling deems my heart in fright
For wolves, that every woodland hind would pass
   And send them snarling back. Yet wolves, fair boy,
   Perchance the more than you such meeting would enjoy!"

   With that she raised her white arms in the wind,
And waving cried aloud. By lonely mere,
   When the night sleep is deep, somewhiles a sound,
   Unearthly and unheavenly, fills the round
Of the starred sky, and earth is filled with fear:
   Such sounds she sent through moonlight and through shade,
   Waving her white arms toward the forest glade;
   And my heart beat beside her, fragrant-skinned.

Three times she called, once to the moony South,
   Once to the mountain woods; and once she turned,
   And where the North Star by his chariot burned,
Once more that strange wail came from that curved mouth:
   And my arms ached her filmy weight to bear,
   And in my blood was tangling all her golden hair.

6

But from the South there came an answering cry
I knew ere yet it ceased. For that reply
   I heard when with my cousins we had found
   A she-wolf in her lair, and on a fire
   Had tied the dam to burn out her desire
   For human flesh, and on the gory ground

Had killed her cubs before her. Then that sound
Had answered the last cry of that sad mother bound;
   And cousins stout cared not to stay and see
   What cheer her spouse should give them; so they ran
   To where were fire and walls and home of man —
   I last — and to my home his foot-tracks followed me.

And from the West there came the fearful wail,
That ever made men's faces change and pale,
  Of the old were-wolf of the woods; that through the dark
  Howled when a man should die. And North again
  A she-wolf screamed like a dead soul in pain: —
    They cried there was a man soon to lie stiff and stark.

7

Once, twice, and thrice they cried; and every cry
Nearer and nearer; and with moonlit eye
  She smiled upon me, mocking. I knew well
  That all in arms I could not fight these foes;
  High to the danger still my courage rose,
    Nor, naked, owned their cries my funeral knell.

I seized her swiftly up from where she stood,
To bear her with me to the angry flood,
  There swim for life or death; face to my face,
  Heart to my heart, breath panting with my breath;
  To live if I could live, die with my death,
    And rot with me in one last long embrace.

"Boy," she laughed, "art afraid of these my friends?
The river but some cowardly mankin sends,
  Who dares not face the forest! Stand your ground:
  I promise you shall have no cause for fear!
  These are my friends whom I have summoned here,
    To do my pleasure fond, to do my bidding bound."

8

"Seal thou thy promise with a kiss!" I cried.
She kissed; — and in my ears murmured the tide,
  And in her eyes the moon and stars were pent,
  And in her lips were past and future bliss,

All life, all thought, sunk in one burning kiss:
  Stars, earth and heaven, in her eyes were blent —

And round the wolves were seated. Panting tongue,
Sharp teeth in cruel jaw, that hungry hung
    Under the gleaming eyes; and all the air
    Was noisome with their scent. The three that cried
    Were foremost; and sat watching, side by side,
      Where first from my young limbs the flesh to tear.

Dark shadows stretched behind them with strange stars
That came and went, as o'er the harbour bars
    The shipman sees the lantern on the shore.
    Dark shadows clustered round upon the grass,
    And backward, forward, would a shadow pass;
      And ever drew they nearer, ever more.

9

We stood, and I stood foremost; till the breath
    Of him from the South whose vixen I had slain,
    Fanned warm on my cold limbs, and a thick rain
Slavered from both those jaws of fearsome death;
    And his coat bristled o'er in lustful hate,
    Big with revenge, and hunger, and my fate.

Yet she behind me gave a silvery laugh,
    Like streamlet on the mountain, rippling clear,
    When first it strikes the tired hunter's ear,
Who turns from summer's hear its rill to quaff.
    Low answered from the pack in fear and dread
    A whine of horror; and uneasy stirred each shadowy head.

She struck her little hand across his ears —
    "Down, rascal! hast no manners for my friend?
    Kiss, dog, where I have kissed." — I saw him bend,

I felt his mouth drip hot and hungry tears
    Over my feet; and then from foot to head
    He slavered me — whose cubs I had laid dead —
    With teeth, and shining eyes, and hair bristling in hate and dread.

10

Ever there rang the silvery laugh behind,
And the eyes of the shadows moved; a single mind
    Seemed to grow into the twining shapeless crowd,
    As they closed together, and closer; poised on their feet,
    As those who wait to know the moment is meet —
    On a sudden the were-wolf rose and howled aloud —

And away to the South were a cloud of galloping backs,
Old dog, were-wolf, and the vixen leading the packs;
    And up the stars rose laughter, awful and shrill:
    She and I were alone. Her parted mouth
    Shrilled, mocking, to the skies; and away to the South
    I saw a rushlight burn in the village under the hill.

O then I turned to her, and I held my eyes
Proud, gazing where I saw her eyelids rise:
    "Now, know you; wolves or fiends, I fear them nought;
    But I will take what heart is in your breast,
    And I will make you follow my behest,
    Natheless for all the spells that e'er were wrought!"

11

Her white hands touched my face. "Poor, gentle boy,
    And have you not enough of Yberha's grace?
    Were you not sated with the wolf's embrace,
That you would know my lips as little coy?
    Would you court a bride who can cast a shade on the sun,
    And will watch the soul in its flight when the rushlight yonder is done?

"I love not ever my father; who reads strange scrolls
  Of how the world shall be happy, and men be kind,
  And great ones from their slaves their chains unbind,
And lowly men be great. I take his rolls
  And read on the other side, of power and pride;
  Who weds must win them for me, whatsoe'er betide.

"Swim home and dream in peace. Not yours to turn
  The forces of the stars out from the sky,
  And wield them; while the men fall down and die
Where'er your finger points, and the worlds burn,
  And horror fills your soul with horror's depth and height,
  And round about you press the forces of the night.

12

"Boy, dare you hold unceasing, endless pain
Thralled in your hand? when a shiver or a stain
  Of fear across your mind would loose it there,
  And in one flood would roll over your brain
  One blank of that unceasing endless pain,
  And agony relentless, and unperishing despair.

"Dare you walk forth on lone eternal hills,
And know beside you lone eternal wills,
  Bend them, unwilling, to tear up the earth,
  To whirl the heavens backward, heap the sea,
  Cast night on noonday, set the Zodiac free.
  And curse a newborn life before its birth?

"Swim home and dream in peace: and woo some girl
Whose charms are blush of cheek, and waft of curl;
  And give her then this kiss." I clasped her form,
  White-robed and slim: "I woo no other maid;
  I fear not death or pain, nor the cold shade
  Of loneliness. Rage all your fiery storm.

13

"Thus I will hold you! And in death or pain,
  Victor or vanquished, till your bosom's snow
  Melt in my heart, I will not let you go:
I will not live away from you again;
  I am more strong than you with all your might,
  And all your beauty is my proper right!"

Still there she stood, clasped closely, dreamingly,
  With moonlit eyes and dewy marble cheek,
  Lips moving not to kiss me or to speak;
Still there she stood, clasped closely, dreamingly.
  Her eyes shone in the darkness, as the light
  That leads forth wanderers, far, far into the night.

Rested her white hand on my hungry arm:
  "And I have been alone; alone," she said;
  "I thought to go alone among the dead,
And lonely guide them with an awful charm.
  I thought alone to turn the weak world's length;
  I knew not that a man had such a strength.

14

"Fold round your arms more closely. How your lip
Is cold, and night-dews from your eyelids drip!
  Fold closely. Now I know that life can give
  Something more sweet than power, yet more sweet
  Than cruelty. Do our hearts together beat?
  To be in lonely strength is not to live.

"Kiss not so close, for I would speak awhile:
Know, love, that I must wander many a mile
  'Twixt now and day. Know, I can never wed,
  Save with death to my lover, but a man

Who knows my every spell to bless or ban;
   Unless I lay all down beside my marriage bed.

"Which will you: wed me as a powerless maid,
Of night, and wolves, and warlock word afraid;
    Or wait till my high art yourself have learned?"
I cried — "I wed no weakling for my bride!
Ride we this rotten world, whate'er betide:
   I kiss you on it." — And her lips like fire burned.

Second Part

15

So three long years I toiled by night and day
To learn her spells. The meteors at play
Cried round us as we sat upon the hills,
The lightning flowed in lucid gentle rills
To bathe her feet; and strange tongues spake anon
Thundering, and red streamers through the welkin shone.

Sometime we pored o'er mystic written signs
Tangled with pictured horrors, wrapt designs
That first were stains of blood upon the page,
And then were men, writhing in pain and rage,
And then shone forth a face in hate and fear,
And grew, until the eyeballs stared as near

As beat her heart to mine. And as we gazed
Sense became dim, and sight and thought amazed:
The walls fell back from out that narrow room,
The world lay wide before us in its gloom,
Strange swift things sped on wings of livid light,
And round about us closed the forces of the night.

16

Sometime from out the shadows of the grave
We called the old Fenickian; who, when wave
Curled o'er his ship to sink it in the deep,
Bade there its mountainous waters hang, asleep
(And still men show it, from the quiet sea
A long white rock, o'erhanging treacherously):

And he would teach us how in Orient land
Great toiling sprites weave cables from the sand;
And he that holds them may chain back the hours
Till his proud life, in ever-waxing powers,
Stretch on a thousand years, and time is tired,
And all lies in his hand that ever he desired:

And how within the bowels of the earth
A fiery race awaits its coming birth,
And they that master mighty spells have care
To say nought that shall break their fetters there;
Else all our world should vanish in a breath,
One fierce and fearsome flame, and long eternal death.

17

And sometime we would pass into the skies
Till the near stars gleamed hotly in her eyes;
And we would look behind the Milky Veil
Where watch the drowsy fates, weary and pale,
Till planets cease to rule. And we would fall
Downward to the abyss from whence the thunders call;

And there were monstrous, mountainous, cloudy forms,
Whose eyes were lightnings, and whose breaths were storms;
Writhing and twisting through the unbounded deep,
Now strove they at their chains, and now would sleep:

When they be loosed the mountains pass to air,
And all the solid earth to windy, dark despair.

And sometime would we sit beneath the trees;
 And I would kiss the blushes to her face,
 And wind her hair in many a wandering grace,
And set it flowing to the evening breeze;
 And bury her with flowers, scenting of spring,
 And hear the white-barred winter-finch his love-bell ring.

Third Part

18

And so there went three years: and I was grown
 Stronger than she, more daring in my spells,
 Calling the spirits of the rugged fells
As shepherd calls his dogs. Our troth was known;
 Merlin would wed Yberha of the Mount,
 Child of the silent man men held of small account.

Yet never had he yielded to our troth,
 Nor ever took her dower at my hand;
 But called me wastrel of an ill-lived land,
Profitless in labour, diligent in sloth,
 No husband for his daughter; but a curse
 To make good bad in her, and make bad worse.

That time the foe came on us. Fiery light
 Shone forth from every hill-top, and all day
 Men drove their women and their herds away,
And digged to wall about them all the night.
 About Yberha's tower they digged the wall;
 Yon moody man was leader of them all.

19

And from the sacred places came a chant
   From daybreak to nightfall; and fierce-eyed priests
   Tore from the rout the best of all the beasts,
Made ox and sheep up the long stoneway pant,
  Till all the altars, set in crimson mire,
  Clouded the sky with smoke and marred the night with fire.

The Prayer of the Priests

Great mountains, hear us!
   Hear us, who deck in flowers your granite brows
   And fill your cups with blood.

Great river, hear us!
   Hear us, who pour our offerings on the wave,
   Whose fairest in thy bosom have their grave.

Sun, hear us!
   We give the best our bitter life allows
   To thee, giver of good.

Gods of the forest, hear us!
   Red drip the branches of your sacred trees:
What other gods there be, O hear us!
   And scent our offerings on the evening breeze.

   Round, round
     We march in mystic rite;
Sound, sound
     The trumpets to the Night:
    She is coming from the east,
    And the sacrifice, O priest,
     Is alight.

Priest of the dawn,
   Is there help?

Priest of the rocks,
    Is there help?
Priest of the flood,
Priest of the wood,
    Is there help?

    Round, round
      We march in mystic rite;
    Sound, sound
      The trumpets to the Night:
      Take our foes, dying deep;
      But we worship thee —
      Let us sleep.

Priest of the Night,
    Is there help?

Yet nearer closed the foe: the holy seers
    Had fled to the holy woods, to pray anew
    In secret caverns where they held the clew;
Our tower rang with lowings, moans, and cheers;
    The strangers were encamped against the wall;
    That, and the moody man, became the hope of all.

Three days they sieged about us; till at length
    We penned the cattle and women in the tower,
    Massed to their weaker wing in all our power,
And rushed to measure with the foe our strength:
    Foremost of all Yberha's father there;
    An axe made like a cross he brandished in the air.

20

Bloodily waged the battle. I was light
Of spear and swift of foot, and through the fight
    Passed like a wandering death. With heavy blows

18

Of axe on target, edgéd stone on hide,
My cousins fought in phalanx, side by side;
   And over all the voice of Yberha's father rose:

"Strike for your children! Strike for love and wife!
Strike for the kindly land that gave you life!
    — O Thou that rulest lives and ways of men,
   Save this poor ignorant people to new days
   That thus a thankful land thy grace repays."
And he struck with the two-edged axe, and cried, "Amen."

But we were few, and I saw Yberha's head at the tower,
And I drew forth, to weave a spell of power
    With her for conquest. Waving hand with hand,
   She on the tower, I back from out the fight,
   We read a twisted spell of potent might
    Pointing to where the crossed axe made a stand; —

21

When all of a sudden the cross flew back as he smote,
Slipping his grasp, and struck me down in the moat,
    I rose with courage strangely faint, a cry
   Rang from the foe; my cousins side by side
   Took blows of axe and spear on the stout bull-hide:
    Yberha's father was down, and our men began to fly.

From out the tower whispered a light footfall,
Where shone my beauty, cold, and white, and tall;
    I leapt quick-hearted o'er our fenceless bank,
   Crying, "Come, sweetheart! speed we to the wood;
   Thy sire is dead: none other ever stood
    To foil our marriage; foiléd spells we well may thank!"

Cold stood she, white and tall. From out the fight
Our men were rallying back upon the right.

She spake: "Take up thy spear and lead the men,
Nor think of spells or love. Sweep back yon foe,
Or never word thine ear from me shall know:
When they are conquered, ask me further then."

22

Dizzy I turned me, and with waving spear
   Called on my men and fell into the press;
   Naught knew I but to long for her caress,
And for her safety to be sick with fear:
   Still with skilled arm I thrust, and thrust again,
   And into the hot foe we fought out way amain.

And as the sun was setting, down the hill
   We pressed them; and my wing the more and more
   Forced them, retreating, to the river shore,
Until they turned to flee, and we to kill:
   But where my cousins stood, stubborn and loud,
   The battle waged like thunder in a thundercloud.

At length there too the foe broke; turned and fled,
   Scattering toward the river, and we ran
   To slay; but my huge cousin, once began
The cloud to break, turned back among the dead,
   And I cried wrathful words; but there they stood,
   While half stricken foe escaped into the flood.

23

We slew till all were fled, or bound, or slain,
Then turned triumphing to the tower again.
   The women busily sped to and fro
   Helping the wounded; or with bitter wail
   Pressed lip to cheek that sundown-light left pale;
   Or vainly, sadly, searched their dead to know.

A Book of Merlin

I was unwounded. Youth, and skill of fence,
And fearless coolness, and a delicate sense
   Of where a man was weakest, kept my head;
  And so, afront of all my lagging men,
  I mounted lightly from the bloody glen,
   And walked to meet my love among the dead.

A dark group stood within our earthen mound;
A body, and my cousins pressing round;
And she, white-robed, the nearest. Lightly treading,
As one that walks from waiting unto wedding,
I came behind her; and, ere I could speak,
Had touched her glossy hair, and kissed her cheek.

24

Like adder coiled about her threatened young,
With head thrown back, and swift death-dealing tongue,
   Turning, she spake: — "Smooth coward! whole of skin,
  You have come well forth from all this bitter strife,
  And saved, at least, one traitorous, worthless life —
   Maid's body, with a weasel's heart within!

"There lies my father, stricken by your guile.
You faced him not to kill him; but, with wile
   Evil and secret, struck him out of sight,
  Spelling I know not what of fatal ban.
  You could lay low a fearless, trustful man,
   Foremost and strongest in his people's fight

"I wed you? Wed me rather to the raven,
Gorged with yon bravest blood, than to a craven."
   With that she faced the rest, and, bowing head —
  "I have been wild and foolish as a maid,
  And tried to learn strange arts, proud not to be afraid:
   For ever now I lay them by," she said.

25

"Worthless they were, worthless I know are those
Who seek out all the thorns whereon the rose
    Of our fair life, by sun and showers fed,
   Blossoms in love and truth. Crook'd thorns there be;
   And strange imaginings those that seek them see:
   Methinks the most of them are false," she said.

"An honest man, with strong and brave right arm
To keep a loving woman from all harm,
    Seeing at night a glowing ingle-bed
   With laughing, dark-haired children, clear of eye,
   Fearlessly helpless, smiling trustfully; —
   Stronger are these than charms or spells," she said.

"Friends, I was wrong; this day I have seen clear
That such things are but vain; be witness here;
    I tell, who know. My days that be unsped
   Henceforth I strive — and what I strive I can —
   To live a woman, as my sire a man,
   Worthy of love from man and child," she said.

26

"This thing that fed my follies, in my blindness
   I thought to marry; but my father wise,
   Seeing my madness with a father's eyes,
Dissuaded, vainly, gently, with a father's kindness.
   — Foolish or false, my strange arts this man shared:
   Traitor in them, his black heart he has bared;

"I leave him, and for ever." Such mad words —
More mad, more fierce than memory affords
    To utter rightly, — with proud head back thrown,
   She uttered; in some glamour, as I thought,

That made her to the bold day I had fought
Blind, and forgetful of our magic throne;

I deemed that it would pass. And cousin stout
Stood forth and said, "Fair lady, in yon rout
   Young Merlin led the van, no traitor he.
  Of star-work tricks I know not; but you twain
  Foolish and young, grow not so young again:
   Marry him, maid! he made our foes to flee."

27

So his two brothers dropped axe-handle down
Upon the ground; and, nodding with wise frown,
   Said, "Aye, the chief is right; he led the van:
  Marry him, lady, 'tis a fightsome lad!"
  And one said, "Lady, be not all so sad;
   Your father breathes, perchance not sped his span."

But she looked on the corse despairingly:
And one said to me, "Lad, 'twere better see
   This is no time for wooing. On the morrow
  She will forget these strange things she has said
  Of all your love-games. Leave her with her dead;
   You must not woo a maiden in her sorrow."

Then looked she on my cousin. Big and tired
He stood, his eye no more with battle fired,
   His face astreak with blood. One ugly gash
  Left half his forehead hanging; his right hand
  Swung powerless, broke at the elbow. Brown and tanned,
   You saw him pale in the lips, and all his eyes with blood asplash.

28

"Friend, you bestrode, untrod, my father's corse

From afternoon till evening. Brave in fight
I knew you; true to what you know is right
I find you: strong and true. For better or worse
   I here do vow me yours. So you me wed
   I will be faithful wife, or know no marriage-bed."

Silence held us, all still. She knelt aground,
   And took his miry, bloodstained hand, and raised
   That ox-hoof to her honeyed lips. Amazed,
I poised my spear; but the brothers held me round.
   Stupid, but not unkindly louts, they bore
   Me, mad with rage, to a coracle on the shore.

And one came with me, sculling where we knew
   Safe cave of refuge. There he stayed with me,
   Lying to watch the water from the sea
Behind the islet where the willow grew;
   And there we stayed a week beside the shore,
   And to this day I never saw her more.

29

For he sailed me down the river, and set me forth
With the fisher-folk that knew us not of the North;
And I flung a stone on his boat as he sailed away
That sank him there, and the tide swept into the bay;
And none knew ever a man had come with me,
Nor boat, nor whence I came, of earth or sky or sea.

I chose me a cave where a wolf had made his den,
And drave them forth with a stick: the people feared me then.
   I lived as the wise men live in Orient lands;
   I made strange spells in the night, and spell on spell
   I learned, till all the world obeyed me well;
   And one, with weaving paces and with waving hands,

You wot of, I made then; and spelled those twain,
Her and her sotted lover, that again
   They ne'er should love, but see me ever there —
  But see me ever betwixt closéd walls,
  Whether, without, sun rises or dew falls,
   Ever in hate, and ever in despair.

30

And I live on in power, power of men,
   To wield their kings and councils, and to wield
   Their herd-like armies on the battle field,
And power o'er all that is beyond their ken.
   And yet, sometimes, when I see the moon in the south,
   Methinks I feel warm lips upon my mouth.

The Prophecies of Merlin, and the Birth of Arthur

King Vortigern the usurper sat upon his throne in London, when, suddenly, upon a certain day, ran in a breathless messenger, and cried aloud—

"Arise, Lord King, for the enemy is come; even Ambrosius and Uther, upon whose throne thou sittest—and full twenty thousand with them—and they have sworn by a great oath, Lord, to slay thee, ere this year be done; and even now they march towards thee as the north wind of winter for bitterness and haste."

At those words Vortigern's face grew white as ashes, and, rising in confusion and disorder, he sent for all the best artificers and craftsmen and mechanics, and commanded them vehemently to go and build him straightway in the furthest west of his lands a great and strong castle, where he might fly for refuge and escape the vengeance of his master's sons—"and, moreover," cried he, "let the work be done within a hundred days from now, or I will surely spare no life amongst you all."

Then all the host of craftsmen, fearing for their lives, found out a proper site whereon to build the tower, and eagerly began to lay in the foundations. But no sooner were the walls raised up above the ground than all their work was overwhelmed and broken down by night invisibly, no man perceiving how, or by whom, or what. And the same thing happening again, and yet again, all the workmen, full of terror, sought out the king, and threw themselves upon their faces before him, beseeching him to interfere and help them or to deliver them from their dreadful work.

Filled with mixed rage and fear, the king called for the astrologers and wizards, and took counsel with them what these things might be, and how to overcome them. The wizards worked their spells and incantations, and in the end declared that nothing but the blood of a youth born without mortal father, smeared on the foundations of the castle, could avail to make it stand. Messengers were therefore sent forthwith through all the land to find, if it were possible, such a child. And, as some of them went down a certain village street, they saw a band of lads fighting and quarrelling, and heard them shout at one—"Avaunt, thou imp!—avaunt! Son of no mortal man! go, find thy father, and leave us in peace."

At that the messengers looked steadfastly on the lad, and asked who he was. One said his name was Merlin; another, that his birth and parentage were known by no man; a third, that the foul fiend alone was his father. Hearing the things, the officers seized Merlin, and carried him before the king by force.

But no sooner was he brought to him than he asked in a loud voice, for what cause he was thus dragged there?

"My magicians," answered Vortigern, "told me to seek out a man that had no human father, and to sprinkle my castle with his blood, that it may stand."

"Order those magicians," said Merlin, "to come before me, and I will convict them of a lie."

The king was astonished at his words, but commanded the magicians to come and sit down before Merlin, who cried to them—

"Because ye know not what it is that hinders the foundation of the castle, ye have advised my blood for a cement to it, as if that would avail; but tell me now rather what there is below that ground, for something there is surely underneath that will not suffer the tower to stand?"

The wizards at these words began to fear, and made no answer. Then said Merlin to the king—

"I pray, Lord, that workmen may be ordered to dig deep down into the ground till they shall come to a great pool of water."

This then was done, and the pool discovered far beneath the surface of the ground.

Then, turning again to the magicians, Merlin said, "Tell me now, false sycophants, what there is underneath that pool?"—but they were silent. Then said he to the king, "Command this pool to be drained, and at the bottom shall be found two dragons, great and huge, which now are sleeping, but which at night awake and fight and tear each other. At their great struggle all the ground shakes and trembles, and so casts down thy towers, which, therefore, never yet could find secure foundations."

The king was amazed at these words, but commanded the pool to be forthwith drained; and surely at the bottom of it did they presently discover the two dragons, fast asleep, as Merlin had declared.

But Vortigern sat upon the brink of the pool till night to see what else would happen.

Then those two dragons, one of which was white, the other red, rose up and came near one another, and began a sore fight, and cast forth fire with their breath. But the white dragon had the advantage, and chased the other to the end of the lake. And he, for grief at his flight, turned back upon his foe, and renewed the combat, and forced him to retire in turn. But in the end the red dragon was worsted, and the white dragon disappeared no man knew where.

When their battle was done, the king desired Merlin to tell him what it meant. Whereat he, bursting into tears, cried out this prophecy, which first foretold the coming of King Arthur.

"Woe to the red dragon, which figureth the British nation, for his banishment cometh quickly; his lurkingholes shall be seized by the white dragon—the Saxon whom thou, O king, hast called to the land. The mountains shall be levelled as the valleys, and the rivers of the valleys shall run blood; cities shall be burned, and churches laid in ruins; till at length the oppressed shall turn for a season and prevail against the strangers. For a Boar of Cornwall shall arise and rend them, and trample their necks beneath his feet. The island shall be subject to his power, and he shall take the forests of Gaul. The house of Romulus shall dread him—all the world shall fear him—and his end shall no man know; he shall be immortal in the mouths of the people, and his works shall be food to those that tell them.

"But as for thee, O Vortigern, flee thou the sons of Constantine, for they shall burn thee in thy tower. For thine own ruin wast thou traitor to their father, and didst bring the Saxon heathens to the land. Aurelius and Uther are even now upon thee to revenge their father's murder; and the brood of the white dragon shall waste thy country, and shall lick thy blood. Find out some refuge, if thou wilt! but who may escape the doom of God?"

The king heard all this, trembling greatly; and, convicted of his sins, said nothing in reply. Only he hasted the builders of his tower by day and night, and rested not till he had fled thereto.

In the meantime, Aurelius, the rightful king, was hailed with joy by the Britons, who flocked to his standard, and prayed to be led against the Saxons. But he, till he had first killed Vortigern, would begin no other war. He marched therefore to Cambria, and came before the tower which the usurper had built. Then, crying out to all his knights, "Avenge ye on him who hath ruined Britain and slain my father and your king!" he rushed with many thousands at the castle walls. But, being driven back again and yet again, at length he thought of fire, and ordered blazing brands to be cast into the building from all sides. These finding soon a proper fuel, ceased not to rage, till spreading to a mighty conflagration, they burned down the tower and Vortigern within it.

Then did Aurelius turn his strength against Hengist and the Saxons, and, defeating them in many places, weakened their power for a long season, so that the land had peace.

Anon the king, making many journeys to and fro, restoring ruined churches and, creating order, came to the monastery near Salisbury, where all those British knights lay buried who had been slain there by the treachery of Hengist. For when in former times Hengist had made a solemn truce with Vortigern, to meet in peace and settle terms, whereby himself and all his Saxons should depart from Britain, the Saxon soldiers carried every one of them beneath his garment a long dagger, and, at a given signal, fell upon the Britons, and slew them, to the number of nearly five hundred.

The sight of the place where the dead lay moved Aurelius to great sorrow, and he cast about in his mind how to make a worthy tomb over so many noble martyrs, who had died there for their country.

When he had in vain consulted many craftsmen and builders, he sent, by the advice of the archbishop, for Merlin, and asked him what to do. "If you would honour the burying-place of these men," said Merlin, "with an everlasting monument, send for the Giants' Dance which is in Killaraus, a mountain in Ireland; for there is a structure of stone there which none of this age could raise without a perfect knowledge of the arts. They are stones of a vast size and wondrous nature, and if they can be placed here as they are there, round this spot of ground, they will stand for ever."

At these words of Merlin, Aurelius burst into laughter, and said, "How is it possible to remove such vast stones from so great a distance, as if Britain, also, had no stones fit for the work?"

"I pray the king," said Merlin, "to forbear vain laughter; what I have said is true, for those stones are mystical and have healing virtues. The giants of old brought them from the furthest coast of Africa, and placed them in Ireland while they lived in that country: and their design was to make baths in them, for use in time of grievous illness. For if they washed the stones and put the sick into the water, it certainly healed them, as also it did them that were wounded in battle; and there is no stone among them but hath the same virtue still."

When the Britons heard this, they resolved to send for the stones, and to make war upon the people of Ireland if they offered to withhold them. So, when they had chosen Uther the king's brother for their chief, they set sail, to the number of 15,000 men, and came to Ireland. There Gillomanius, the king, withstood them fiercely, and not till after a great battle could they approach the Giants' Dance, the sight of which filled them with joy and admiration. But when they sought to move the stones, the strength of all the army was in vain, until Merlin, laughing at their failures, contrived machines of wondrous cunning, which took them down with ease, and placed them in the ships.

When they had brought the whole to Salisbury, Aurelius, with the crown upon his head, kept for four days the feast of Pentecost with royal pomp; and in the midst of all the clergy and the people, Merlin raised up the stones, and set them round the sepulchre of the knights and barons, as they stood in the mountains of Ireland.

Then was the monument called "Stonehenge," which stands, as all men know, upon the plain of Salisbury to this very day.

Soon thereafter it befell that Aurelius was slain by poison at Winchester, and was himself buried within the Giants' Dance.

At the same time came forth a comet of amazing size and brightness, darting out a beam, at the end whereof was a cloud of fire shaped like a dragon, from whose mouth went out two rays, one stretching over Gaul, the other ending in seven lesser rays over the Irish sea.

At the appearance of this star a great dread fell upon the people, and Uther, marching into Cambria against the son of Vortigern, himself was very troubled to learn what it might mean. Then Merlin, being called before him, cried with a loud voice: "O mighty loss! O stricken Britain! Alas! the great prince is gone from us. Aurelius Ambrosius is dead, whose death will be ours also, unless God help us. Haste, therefore, noble Uther, to destroy the enemy; the victory shall be thine, and thou shalt be king of all Britain. For the star with the fiery dragon signifies thyself; and the ray over Gaul portends that thou shalt have a son, most mighty, whom all those kingdoms shall obey which the ray covers."

Thus, for the second time, did Merlin foretell the coming of King Arthur. And Uther, when he was made king, remembered Merlin's words, and caused two dragons to be made in gold, in likeness of the dragon he had seen in the star. One of these he gave to Winchester Cathedral, and had the other carried into all his wars before him, whence he was ever after called Uther Pendragon, or the dragon's head.

Now, when Uther Pendragon had passed through all the land, and settled it—and even voyaged into all the countries of the Scots, and tamed the fierceness of that rebel people—he came to London, and ministered justice there. And it befell at a certain great banquet and high feast which the king made at Easter-tide, there came, with many other earls and barons, Gorloïs, Duke of Cornwall, and his wife Igerna, who was the most famous beauty in all Britain. And soon thereafter, Gorloïs being slain in battle, Uther determined to make Igerna his own wife. But in order to do this, and enable him to come to her—for she was shut up in the high castle of Tintagil, on the furthest coast of Cornwall—the king sent for Merlin, to take counsel with him and to pray his help. This, therefore, Merlin promised him on one condition—namely, that the king should give him up the first son born of the marriage. For Merlin by his arts foreknew that this firstborn should be the long-wished prince, King Arthur.

When Uther, therefore, was at length happily wedded, Merlin came to the castle on a certain day, and said, "Sir, thou must now provide thee for the nourishing of thy child."

And the king, nothing doubting, said, "Be it as thou wilt."

"I know a lord of thine in this land," said Merlin, "who is a man both true and faithful; let him have the nourishing of the child. His name is Sir Ector, and he hath fair possessions both in England and in Wales. When, therefore, the child is born, let him be delivered unto me, unchristened, at yonder postern-gate, and I will bestow him in the care of this good knight."

So when the child was born, the king bid two knights and two ladies to take it, bound in rich cloth of gold, and deliver it to a poor man whom they should discover at the postern-gate. And the child being delivered thus to Merlin, who himself took the guise of a poor man, was carried by him to a holy priest and christened by the name of Arthur, and then was taken to Sir Ector's house, and nourished at Sir Ector's wife's own breasts. And in the same house he remained privily for many years, no man soever knowing where he was, save Merlin and the king.

Anon it befell that the king was seized by a lingering distemper, and the Saxon heathens, taking their occasion, came back from over sea, and swarmed upon the land, wasting it with fire and sword. When Uther heard thereof, he fell into a greater rage than his weakness could bear, and commanded all his nobles to come before him, that he might upbraid them for their cowardice. And when he had sharply and hotly rebuked them, he swore that he himself, nigh unto death although he lay, would lead them forth against the enemy. Then causing a horse-litter to be made, in which he might be carried—for he was too faint and weak to ride—he went up with all his army swiftly against the Saxons.

But they, when they heard that Uther was coming in a litter, disdained to fight with him, saying it would be shame for brave men to fight with one half dead. So they retired into their city; and, as it were in scorn of danger, left the gates wide open. But Uther straightway commanding his men to assault the town, they did so without loss of time, and had already reached the gates, when the Saxons, repenting too late of their haughty pride, rushed forth to the defence. The battle raged till night, and was begun again next day; but at last, their leaders, Octa and Eosa, being slain, the Saxons turned their backs and fled, leaving the Britons a full triumph.

The king at this felt so great joy, that, whereas before he could scarce raise himself without help, he now sat upright in his litter by himself, and said, with a laughing and merry face, "They called me the half-dead king, and so indeed I was; but victory to me half dead is better than defeat and the best health. For to die with honour is far better than to live disgraced."

But the Saxons, although thus defeated, were ready still for war. Uther would have pursued them; but his illness had by now so grown, that his knights and barons kept him from the adventure. Whereat the enemy took courage, and left nothing undone to destroy the land; until, descending to the vilest treachery, they resolved to kill the king by poison.

To this end, as he lay sick at Verulam, they sent and poisoned stealthily a spring of clear water, whence he was wont to drink daily; and so, on the very next day, he was taken with the pains of death, as were also a hundred others after him, before the villainy was discovered, and heaps of earth thrown over the well.

The knights and barons, full of sorrow, now took counsel together, and came to Merlin for his help to learn the king's will before he died, for he was by this time speechless. "Sirs, there is no remedy," said Merlin, "and God's will must be done; but be ye all to-morrow before him, for God will make him speak before he die."

So on the morrow all the barons, with Merlin, stood round the bedside of the king; and Merlin said aloud to Uther, "Lord, shall thy son Arthur be the king of all this realm after thy days?"

Then Uther Pendragon turned him about, and said, in the hearing of them all, "God's blessing and mine be upon him. I bid him pray for my soul, and also that he claim my crown, or forfeit all my blessing;" and with those words he died.

Then came together all the bishops and the clergy, and great multitudes of people, and bewailed the king; and carrying his body to the convent of Ambrius, they buried it close by his brother's grave, within the "Giants' Dance."

Merlin

Of Merlin and how he served King Arthur, something has been already shown. Loyal he was ever to Uther Pendragon and to his son, King Arthur, and for the latter especially he wrought great marvels. He brought the King to his rights; he made him his ships; and some say that Camelot, with its splendid halls, where Arthur would gather his knights around him at the great festivals of the year, at Christmas, at Easter, and at Pentecost, was raised by his magic, without human toil. Bleise, the aged magician who dwelt in Northumberland and recorded the great deeds of Arthur and his knights, had been Merlin's master in magic; but it came to pass in time that Merlin far excelled him in skill, so that his enemies declared no mortal was his father, and called him devil's son.

Then, on a certain time, Merlin said to Arthur: "The time draws near when ye shall miss me, for I shall go down alive into the earth; and it shall be that gladly would ye give your lands to have me again." Then Arthur was grieved, and said: "Since ye know your danger, use your craft to avoid it." But Merlin answered: "That may not be."

Now there had come to Arthur's court, a damsel of the Lady of the Lake—her whose skill in magic, some say, was greater than Merlin's own; and the damsel's name was Vivien. She set herself to learn the secrets of Merlin's art, and was ever with him, tending upon the old man and, with gentleness and tender service, winning her way to his heart; but all was a pretence, for she was weary of him and sought only his ruin, thinking it should be fame for her, by any means whatsoever, to enslave the greatest wizard of his age. And so she persuaded him to pass with her overseas into King Ban's land of Benwick, and there, one day, he showed her a wondrous rock, formed by magic art. Then she begged him to enter into it, the better to declare to her its wonders; but when once he was within, by a charm that she had learnt from Merlin's self, she caused the rock to shut down that never again might he come forth. Thus was Merlin's prophecy fulfilled, that he should go down into the earth alive. Much they marvelled in Arthur's court what had become of the great magician, till on a time, there rode past the stone a certain Knight of the Round Table and heard Merlin lamenting his sad fate. The knight would have striven to raise the mighty stone, but Merlin bade him not waste his labour, since none might release him save her who had imprisoned him there. Thus Merlin passed from the world through the treachery of a damsel, and thus Arthur was without aid in the days when his doom came upon him.

The Prophecy of Merlin

For three long nights had King Arthur watch'd,
The light from the turret shone!
For three long nights had King Arthur wak'd,
He pass'd them all alone!

On the fourth, at the first hour's summon bell,
As the warder walk'd his round,
A figure cross'd at the postern gate,
That enters underground;

All wrapt it was in a monkish cowl,
By the gate-lamp burning dim,
When a double shadow slid across,
And another stood by him!

In low and broken tones they spoke,
Till the fourth hour ceas'd to ring:
That monk had Merlin's giant form,
The other was the king.

The morning shone on Camlan hills,
And the summon horn was blown;
But not a knight would mount the tow'r
Where Arthur watch'd alone!

When noon was past, the king came down,
He bore his dragon shield;
And dark and dread was his clouded brow,
On the eve of Camlan field!

Slowly past that fateful eve,
And sad it wore away;
And sad and silent was the king
As he watch'd the break of day;

All down the slope of Camlan hill,
And along the river's side,

The Great Book of Merlin

The rebel bands were posted round,
Since the fall of eventide:

From the signal posts the shout begins,
When the sky was bright and clear;
And the red sun shone on the steel dragon,
On King Arthur's standard-spear!

Above the rest was Britain's crest
In living flame enroll'd!
And the Virgin's form, in silver wrought,
With the brazon dragon bold!

O! in the field of Camlan fight,
Ere the burning noon was o'er,
The red blood ran, like a river-wave,
On the dry and parched shore:

King Arthur spurr'd his foaming horse
Amid that living flood!
And twice he wav'd his witched sword
Where the dauntless Modred stood!

But who could stand by Arthur's side,
When that steel of terror shone?
When the fire of wroth was in his eye,
And he rais'd his arm alone!

That sun that blaz'd in middle sky,
And flam'd on hill and dell;
Its westering light had sunk in night,
When the mighty Modred fell!

But the blood that flows is Arthur's blood,
His fiery eye is dim!
And a dew like death is on his face,
And over every limb!

A Book of Merlin

He lean'd him down on his dragon shield,
He clasp'd his beaver on!
And the gushing blood it ceas'd at once,
But they heard no dying groan.

O! how they strove till the night came on,
And all to raise that masque again!
And every arm by turns had tried,
But every arm was vain!

They held him in their arms, and wept
With tears of deep despair!
Till they fear'd to touch that plate armour,
For the sound was hollow there!

Then they drew that witched sword,
And they heard the armour ring!
They wav'd it twice in Merlin's name
Before they touch'd the king.

At once the cross-lace open'd wide,
They felt the rushing air!
But that mail was hollow as the grave,
Nor form, nor body there.

As wild they gaz'd, the iron rings
Were clasped as before!
But the tongue that call'd on Merlin's name
Was dumb for ever more!

Mean time, the king was borne away,
In deep and death-like sleep the while,
To the charmed sea, by magic spell,
By the Queen of the Yellow Isle!

And when his tranced soul was rous'd,
He thought, and thought how this might be,
For there was nought but sea and sky

As far as he could see.

King Arthur gaz'd on the calmed surge,
So clear beyond compare!
But neither the form of living man,
Nor the sound of life was there:

The ship it mov'd on the sleeping wave
Like a bird upon the air;
He knew it gained on the deep,
But he felt no motion there!

O, then! he had no trace of time
How long he was on that pathless sea!
But he could have rested there for aye,
So sweet it seem'd to be!

How many times he watch'd the sun,
And saw it sink, he never knew;
For it ne'er was more than faint twilight
In that sky of stainless blue!

Ah! then he thought, within that ship
He ever more was doom'd to be!
And he had not once bethought him yet
Of Merlin's prophecy!

Those sleepless nights he watch'd alone,
When the damps of midnight fell!
That voice, of more than human tone,
He heard in Merlin's cell;

That night, the eve of Camlan fight,
When he felt his courage fail;
When the chill of death was on his brow,
Like a bloodless vision pale;

That night, his knocking knees refus'd

To bear him from the cave;
When, press'd in his, the hand of blood
Its deadly pressure gave!

Clear was the sky, and O! with this
What summer could compare?
What woes could press on Arthur's heart,
When he breath'd that blessed air?

Clear was the sky! the ship drew near
Without the aid of wind or toil!
And, lighted by the morning sun,
He saw the charmed Isle!

The ship was steady on her keel,
Wash'd by that soft and lovely flood;
And, blushing, on the yellow beach,
The Queen of Beauty stood.

High in one hand, of snowy white,
A cup of sparkling pearl she bore;
And she reach'd it to the tranced king
As he knelt upon the shore:

All pallid now was Arthur's brow,
While he took the draught she gave;
For he thought on what the hand of blood
Had mingled in the cave:

He thought on what the fiend pronounc'd,
That Merlin's spirit brought;
And he fix'd his eyes on that ladie's face,
And trembled at the thought.

Ah! in these eyes, of softest blue,
What magic dwells, to lull the soul!
And Arthur saw their mild reproach,
And rais'd the fraughted bowl!

The Great Book of Merlin

His lips have drain'd that sparkling cup,
And he turn'd on her his raptur'd eyes!
When something, like a demon-smile,
Betray'd the smooth disguise!

He started up! he call'd aloud!
And, wild, survey'd her as she stood:
When she rais'd aloof the other arm,
And he knew the hand of blood!

The voice, that answer'd to his call,
Was that he heard within the cave!
When the mighty form of Urien
Was roused from the grave!

It told him, that the hour was come
He too must slumber in the cave;
When nought would reach his burial-place,
But the murmurs of the wave!

It told him of the years to pass
Before his kingdom he could see:
And Arthur knew he would return,
From Merlin's prophecy.

King Arthur's body was not found,
Nor ever laid in holy grave:
And nought has reach'd his burial-place,
But the murmurs of the wave.

The Wisdom of Merlyn

These are the time-words of Merlyn, the voice of his age recorded,
  All his wisdom of life, the fruit of tears in his youth, of joy in his
manhood hoarded,
  All the wit of his years unsealed, to the witless alms awarded.

*

These are his time-gifts of song, his help to the heavy-laden,
  Words of an expert of life, who has gathered its sins in his sack, its
virtues to grieve and gladden,
  Speaking aloud as one who is strong to the heart of man, wife and
maiden.

*

For he is Merlyn of old, the once young, the still robed in glory,
  Ancient of days though he be, with wisdom only for wealth and the
crown of his locks grown hoary,
  Yet with the rage of his soul untamed, the skill of his lips in story.

*

He dares not unhouselled die, who has seen, who has known, who has
tasted
  What of the splendours of Time, of the wise wild joys of the Earth, of the
newness of pleasures quested,
  All that is neither of then nor now, Truth's naked self clean-breasted,

*

Things of youth and of strength, the earth with its infinite pity,
  Glories of moutain and plain, of streams that wind from the hills to the
insolent human city,
  Dark with its traders of human woe enthroned in the seats of the mighty.

*

Fair things nobler than Man before the day of his ruling,
  Free in their ancient peace, ere he came to change, to destroy, to hinder
with his schooling,
  Asking naught that was his to give save freedom from his fooling.

*

Beautiful, wonderful, wise, a consonant law-ruled heaven,
  Garden ungardened yet, in need yet hardly of God to walk there noon
or even,
  Beast and bird and flower in its place, Earth's wonders more than seven.

*

Of these he would speak and confess, to the young who regard not their heirship,

Of beauty to boys who are blind, of might to the impotent strong, to the women who crowd Time's fair ship,

Of pearls deep hid in Love's Indian seas, the name of the God they worship.

*

Thus let it be with Merlyn before his daylight is ended,

One last psalm of his life, the light of it lipped with laughter, the might of it mixed and blended

Still with the subtle sweet need of tears than Pleasure's self more splendid,

*

Psalm and hymn of the Earth expounding what Time teaches,

Creed no longer of wrath, of silent issueless hopes, of a thing which beyond Man's reach is,

Hope deferred till the heart grows sick, while the preacher vainly preaches.

*

Nay but a logic of life, which needeth no deferring,

Life with its birthright love, the sun the wind and the rain in multiple pleasure stirring

Under the summer leaves at noon, with no sad doubt of erring.

*

No sad legend of sin, since his an innocent Eden

Is, and a garden of grace, its gateway clear of the sword, its alleys not angel-ridden,

Its tree of life at the lips of all and never a fruit forbidden.

*

Merlyn is no vain singer to vex men's ears in the street,

Nay, nor a maid's unbidden. He importuneth none with his song, be it never so wild and sweet.

She that hath ears to hear, let her hear; he will not follow her feet.

*

Merlyn makes no petition. He asketh of no man alms.

Prince and prophet is he, a monarch, a giver of gifts, a lord of the open palms,

Sueth he naught, not at God's own hand, though he laudeth the Lord in
psalms.

*

Merlyn would speak his message only to hearts that are strong,
 To him that hath courage to climb, who would gather time's samphire
flowers, who would venture the crags among.
 To her who would lesson her soul to fear, with love for sermon and song.

*

Merlyn hath arms of pity, the weak he would hold to his soul,
 Make them partakers of truth, of the ancient weal of the Earth, of the
life-throb from Pole to Pole.
 He would hold them close; he would dry their tears; with a kiss he would
make them whole.

*

Thus would he sing and to thee, thou child with the eyes of passion
 Watching his face in the dark, in the silent light of the stars, while he
in his godlike fashion
 Maketh his mock at the fears of men, nor spareth to lay the lash on.

*

Thus would thy Merlyn devise, ere the days of his years be numbered,
 Now at threescore and ten. He would leave his word to the world, his
soul of its load uncumbered.
 Then would he lay his ear to the grave, and sleep as his childhood
slumbered.

*

What is the fruit of Wisdom? To learn the proportion of things;
 To know the ant from the lion, the whale from the crest of the wave,
the ditty the grasshopper sings
 From the chaunt of the full-fledged Paradise bird as he shakes the dew
from his wings.

*

There is one thing more than knowledge, a harvest garnered by few:
 To tutor the heart to achieve, to fashion the act to the hand, to do and
not yearn to do,
 To say to the wish of the soul "I will," to have gathered the flower where
it grew.

*

I was young, and they told me "Tarry. The rash in the nets are taken.

If there be doubt of thy deed, abstain, lest the day of danger behold thee by these forsaken,

Lest thou lie in the lion's den thou hast roused, with the eyes thou hast dared to waken.

*

They spake, but I answered "Nay, who waiteth shall take no quarry.

Pleasure is fleet as the roe; in the vales he feedeth to-day, but at night when the eyes grow weary

Lo, he hath passed to the desolate hills; he is gone. Nay, he may not tarry."

*

For Joy too needeth a net. He cometh tame to thy hand,

Asketh an alms of thy life, to serve thee, thy jubilant slave, if thou wouldst but understand.

Then is thy moment, O Man, for the noose, be it steel or a silken band.

*

Therefore, where doubt is, do! Thou shalt stumble in thine endeavour

Ay, till thy knees be sore, thy back with the arrows of grief, and thou stand with an empty quiver.

Yet shall thy heart prevail through its pain, for pain is a mastering lever.

*

Wouldst thou be wise, O Man? At the knees of a woman begin.

Her eyes shall teach thee thy road, the worth of the thing called pleasure, the joy of the thing called sin.

Else shalt thou go to thy grave in pain for the folly that might have been.

*

For know, the knowledge of women the beginning of wisdom is.

Who had seven hundred wives and concubines hundreds three, as we read in the book of bliss?

Solomon, wisest of men and kings, and "all of them princesses."

*

Yet, be thou stronger than they. To be ruled of a woman is ill.

Life hath an hundred ways, beside the way of her arms, to give thee of joy thy fill.

Only is love of thy life the flower. Be thine the ultimate will.

*

A right way is to be happy, a wrong way too. Then beware.

Leave the colt in his stall, he shall grow to a thankless jade, be he never so fat and fair.

Sloth is a crime. Rise up, young fool, and grasp thy joy by the hair.

*

What is the motto of youth? There is only one. Be thou strong.

Do thy work and achieve, with thy brain, with thy hands, with thy heart, the deeds which to strength belong.

Strike each day thy blow for the right, or failing strike for the wrong.

*

He that would gain let him give. The shut hand hardly shall win.

Open thy palms to the poor, O thou of the indigent heart. There shall pleasure be poured therein.

Use thy soul to the cord of joy. If thou sin must, strongly sin.

*

Cast thy whole heart away. The Earth, philosophers tell,

Leaps to a pebble thrown, be it never so little; it moved to the bidding of that which fell.

Throw thy heart! Thou shalt move the world, though thou fall on the floor of Hell.

*

Few have the courage of loving. Faint hearts! The loss is theirs.

Few of their idlest whims. "I would win to Rome ere I die," one cried in his daily cares,

Yet plods on on 'Change to his grave, the slave of his stocks and shares.

*

Learn to appraise thy desires, to weigh the wares of thy heart.

If thou wouldst play with pleasure, avoid Love's passionate tides, its perilous Ocean chart,

Hug the shores of Love's inland seas, and buy thy joys in the mart.

*

Love lightly, but marry at leisure. Wild Love is a flower of the field

Waiting all hands to gather and ours. If we leave it another will win it and kneel where we kneeled.

Marriage is one tame garden rose in a garden fenced and sealed.

*

O thou who art sitting silent! Youth, with the eyelids of grief!

How shall I rouse thee to wit? Thou hast stolen the joy of our world. Thou scornest its vain relief.

Nay, she is here. Be thy tongue set free. Play up, thou eloquent thief.
*

Doubt not thy absolution, sinner, who darest to sin.
So thou prevail in the end, she shall hold thee guiltless of guile, a hero,
a paladin.
The end in her eyes hath thee justified, whatever thy means have been.
*

Love is of body and body, the physical passion of joy;
The desire of the man for the maid, her nakedness strained to his own;
the mother's who suckles her boy
With the passionate flow of her naked breast. All else is a fraudulent toy.
*

Of the house where Love is the master thy beauty may hold the key.
It shall open the hall-door wide, shout loud thy name to its lord. Yet,
wouldst thou its full guest be,
Bring with thee other than beauty, wit. Then sit at the feast made free.
*

"To talk of love is to make love." Truly, a maxim of price.
Nathless the noblest soul, shouldst thou tell her of passionate things and
fail to gaze in her eyes,
Shall hold thee cheap in her woman's pride, a clown for thy courtesies.
*

Love hath two mountain summits, the first where pleasure was born
Faint in the cloud-land of light, a vision of possible hope; the second a
tempest-torn
Crag where passion is lord and king. Betwixt them what vales forlorn!
*

Happiness needs to be learned. In youth the ideal woman
Gazed at afar was a dream, a priceless untouchable prize, while she in
your arms, too human,
Mocked you with love. 'Tis an art learned late; alas, and the whole by no
man.
*

O! thou in the purple gendered. Thou needst pain for thy case.
Lose thy health or thy heart. Be bowed in thy soul's despond. Be
whelmed in a world's disgrace.
So shall thy eyes be unsealed of pride and see Love face to face.
*

46

If thou wouldst win love, speak. She shall read the truth on thy lips.

Spoken vows shall prevail, the spell of thy eloquent hand, the flame of thy finger-tips.

Write? She is reading another's eyes while thy sad pen dips and dips.

*

Thou hast ventured a letter of passion, in ease of thy passionate heart?

Nay, be advised; there is fear, mischance in the written word, when lovers are far apart.

Pain is betrayed by the subtle pen where lips prevailed without art.

*

Love is fire. In the lighting, it raiseth a treacherous smoke,

Telling its tale to the world; but anon, growing clear in its flame, may be hid by an old wife's cloak,

And the world learn nothing more and forget the knowledge its smouldering woke.

*

Comes there a trouble upon thee? Be silent, nor own the debt.

Friendship kicks at the goad; thy naked state is its shame; thou hast angered these with thy fret.

Wait. The world shall forgive thy sin. It asks but leave to forget.

*

The world is an indolent house-shrew. It scolds but cares not to know

Whether in fancy or fact. What it thinks we have done, that it scourges; the true thing we did it lets go.

What matter? We fare less ill than our act, ay, all of us; more be our woe!

*

There were days when wisdom is witless, when folly is noble, sublime.

Let us thank the dear gods for our madness, the rush of the blood in our veins, the exuberant pulsings of Time,

And pray, while we sin the forbidden sin, we be spared our penance of crime.

*

There are habits and customs of passion. Long loves are a tyrannous debt.

But to some there is custom of change, the desire of the untrodden ways, with sunshine of days that were wet,

Of the four fair wives of love's kindly law by licence of Mahomet.

*

Experience all is of use, save one, to have angered a friend.

Break thy heart for a maid; another shall love thee anon. The gold shall return thou didst spend,

Ay, and thy beaten back grow whole. But friendship's grave is the end.

*

Why do I love thee, brother? We have shared what things in our youth,

Battle and siege and triumph, together, always together, in wanderings North and South.

But one thing shared binds nearer than all, the kisses of one sweet mouth.

*

He that hath loved the mother shall love the daughter no less,

Sister the younger sister. There are tones how sweet to his ear, gestures that plead and press,

Echoes fraught with remembered things that cry in the silences.

*

Fly from thy friend in his fortune, his first days of wealth, of fame;

Or, if thou needest to meet him, do thou as the children of Noah, walk backwards and guard thee from blame.

He who saw found forgiveness none. With thee it were haply the same.

*

Bridegroom, thy pride is unseemly. Thou boastest abroad, with a smile,

Thou hast read our humanity's riddle. Nay, wait yet a year with thy bride; she shall lesson thee wiser the while.

Then shalt thou blush for thy words to-day, the shame of thy innocent guile.

*

The love of a girl is a taper lit on a windy night.

Awhile it lightens our darkness, consoles with its pure sudden flame, and the shadows around it grow white.

Anon with a rain-gust of tears it is gone, and we blink more blind for the light.

*

Sage, thou art proud of thy knowledge, what mountains and marvels seen!

Thou hast loved how madly, how often! hast known what wiles of the heart, what ways of maid, wife and quean!

Yet shalt thou still be betrayed by love, befooled like a boy on the green.

*

Oh, there is honour in all love. Have lips once kissed thee, be dumb,
Save in their only praise. To cheapen the thing thou hast loved is to bite
at thyself thy thumb,
To shout thy own fool's fault to the world, and beat thy shame on a
drum.

*

Who hath dared mock at thy beauty, Lady? Who deemeth thee old?
If he had seen thee anon in the tender light of thine eyes, as I saw thee,
what tales had he told
Of ruined kingdoms and kings for one, of misers spending their gold!

*

Friendship or Love? You ask it: which binds with the stronger tether?
Friendship? Thy comrade of youth, who laughed with thee on thy road?
What ailed him in that rough weather,
When to thy bosom Love's angel crept, twin tragedies locked together?

*

Friendship is fostered with gifts. Be it so; little presents? Yes.
Friendship! But ah, not Love, since love is itself Love's gift and it
angereth him to have less.
Woe to the lover who dares to bring more wealth than his tenderness.

*

This to the woman: Forbear his gifts, the man's thou wouldst hold.
Cheerfully he shall give and thou nothing guess, yet anon he shall weigh
thee in scales of his gold.
Woe to thee then if the charge be more than a heartache's cost all told.

*

Thou art tempted, a passion unworthy? Long struggle hath dulled thy
brain?
How shalt thou save thee, poor soul? How buy back the peace of thy
days? If of rest thou be fain,
Oft is there virtue in yielding all; thou shalt not be tempted again.

*

Sacrifice truly is noble. Yet, Lady, ponder thy fate.
Many a victory, won in tears by her who forbore, hath ruined her soul's
estate.
Virtue's prize was too dear a whim, the price agreed to too great.

*

Virtue or vice? Which, think you, should need more veil for her face?

49

Virtue hath little fear; she goeth in unchaste guise; she ventureth all disgrace.

Poor Vice hid in her shame sits dumb while a stranger taketh her place.

*

Chastity? Who is unchaste? The church-wed wife, without blame

Yielding her body nightly, a lack-love indolent prize, to the lord of her legal shame?

Or she, the outlawed passionate soul? Their carnal act is the same.

*

Whence is our fountain of tears? We weep in childhood for pain,

Anon for triumph in manhood, the sudden glory of praise, the giant mastered and slain.

Age weeps only for love renewed and pleasure come back again.

*

What is our personal self? A fading record of days

Held in our single brain, memory linked with memory back to our childhood's ways.

Beyond it what? A tradition blurred of gossip and nursemaid says.

*

Why dost thou plain of thine age, O thou with the beard that is thin?

Art thou alone in thy home? Is there none at thy side, not one, to deem thee a man among men?

Nay, thou art young while she holds thy hand, be thy years the threescore and ten.

*

The world is untimely contrived. It gives us our sunshine in summer,

Its laughing face in our youth, when we need it not to be gay, being each one his own best mummer.

All its frown is for life that goes, its smile for the last new comer.

*

Europe a horologe is, ill mounted and clogged with grime,

Asia a clock run down. Its hands on the dial are still; its hours are told by no chime.

Nathless, twice in the twenty-four, it shall tell thee exactly the time.

*

What is the profit of knowledge? Ah none, though to know not is pain!

We grieve like a child in the dark; we grope for a chink at the door, for a way of escape from the chain;

We beat on life's lock with our bleeding hands, till it opens. And where is the gain?

*

I have tried all pleasures but one, the last and sweetest; it waits.

Childhood, the childhood of age, to totter again on the lawns, to have done with the loves and the hates,

To gather the daisies, and drop them, and sleep on the nursing knees of Fates.

*

I asked of the wise man "Tell me, what age is the age of pleasure?

Twenty years have I lived. I have spread my meshes in vain. I have taken a paltry treasure.

Where is the heart of the gold?" And he, "I will tell thee anon at leisure."

*

I pleaded at thirty "Listen. I have played, I have lost, I have won.

I have loved in joy and sorrow. My life is a burden grown with the thought of its sands outrun.

Where is the joy of our years? At forty? "Say it is just begun."

*

At forty I made love's mourning. I stood alone with my foes,

Foot to fooot with my Fate, as a man at grips with a man, returning blows for blows

In the joy of battle "'Tis here" I cried. But the wise man, "Nay, who knows?"

*

At fifty I walked sedately. At sixty I took my rest.

I had learned the good with the evil. I troubled my soul no more, I had reached the Isles of the Blest.

The sage was dead who had warned my fears. I was wise, I too, with the best.

*

What do we know of Being? Our own? How short lived, how base!

That which is not our own? The eternal enrolment of stars, the voids and the silences!

The enormous might of the mindless globes whirling through infinite space!

*

The infinite Great overhead, the infinite Little beneath!
The turn of the cellular germ, the giddy evolving of life in the intricate struggle for breath,
The microbe, the mote alive in the blood, the eyeless atom of death!

*

Yet which is the greater Being? We have dreamed of a life-giving God,
Him, the mind of the Sun, the conscious brain-flower of Space, with a cosmic form and abode,
With thought and pity and power of will, Humanity's ethical code.

*

We have dreamed, but we do not believe. Be He here, be He not, 'tis as one.
His Godhead, how does it help? He is far. He is blind to our need. Nay, nay, He is less than the Sun,
Less than the least of the tremulous stars, than our old scorned idols of stone.

*

For He heareth not, nor seeth. As we to the motes in our blood,
So is He to our lives, a possible symbol of power, a formula half understood.
But the voice of Him, where? the hand grip, where? A child's cry lost in a wood.

*

Therefore is Matter monarch, the eternal the infinite Thing,
The "I that am" which reigneth, which showeth no shadow of change, while humanities wane and spring,
Which saith "Make no vain Gods before me, who only am Lord and King."

*

What then is Merlyn's message, his word to thee weary of pain,
Man, on thy desolate march, thy search for an adequate cause, for a thread, for a guiding rein,
Still in the maze of thy doubts and fears, to bring thee thy joy again?

*

Thou hast tried to climb to the sky; thou hast called it a firmament;
Thou hast found it a thing infirm, a heaven which is no haven, a bladder punctured and rent,
A mansion frail as the rainbow mist, as thy own soul impotent.

*

Thou hast clung to a dream in thy tears; thou hast stayed thy rage with a hope;

Thou hast anchored thy wreck to a reed, a cobweb spread for thy sail, with sand for thy salvage rope;

Thou hast made thy course with a compass marred, a toy for thy telescope.

*

What hast thou done with thy days? Bethink thee, Man, that alone,

Thou of all sentient things, hast learned to grieve in thy joy, hast earned thee the malison

Of going sad without cause of pain, a weeper and woe-begone.

*

Why? For the dream of a dream of another than this fair life

Joyous to all but thee, by every creature beloved in its spring-time of passion rife,

By every creature but only thee, sad husband with sadder wife,

*

Scared at thought of the end, at the simple logic of death,

Scared at the old Earth's arms outstretched to hold thee again, thou child of an hour, of a breath,

Seeking refuge with all but her, the mother that comforteth.

*

Merlyn's message is this: he would bid thee have done with pride.

What has it brought thee but grief, thy parentage with the Gods, thy kinship with beasts denied?

What thy lore of a life to come in a cloud-word deified?

*

O thou child which art Man, distraught with a shadow of ill!

O thou fool of thy dreams, thou gatherer rarely of flowers but of fungi of evil smell,

Poison growths of the autumn woods, rank mandrake and mort-morell!

*

Take thy joy with the rest, the bird, the beast of the field,

Each one wiser than thou, which frolic in no dismay, which seize what the seasons yield,

And lay thee down when thy day is done content with the unrevealed.

*

Take the thing which thou hast. Forget thy kingdom unseen.

Lean thy lips on the Earth; she shall bring new peace to thy eyes with her healing vesture green.

Drink once more at her fount of love, the one true hippocrene.

*

O thou child of thy fears! Nay, shame on thy childish part

Weeping when called to thy bed. Take cheer. When the shadows come, when the crowd is leaving the mart,

Then shalt thou learn that thou needest sleep, Death's kindly arms for thy heart.

Wise Merlin's Foolishness

Arthur was now established as king over all the land. The great council hall at Camelot, that is Winchester, had been built, some say by Merlin's skill; and the most loyal and the bravest knights of the world had been gathered at Arthur's court to do honour to him and his fair Queen Guenever.

Merlin was Arthur's wisest helper and most powerful friend, as he had before been the helper and friend of his father Uther, for whom he had made the Round Table, signifying the roundness of the world. We have seen how he hid the young Arthur away from the jealousy of the wild barons, and how, by his power over men and his knowledge of what would be, he had saved the King's life and guided his wise rule. The old magician Bleise, that dwelt in Northumberland, was Merlin's master, and he it was that wrote down all the battles of Arthur with his enemies word by word as Merlin told him, and all the battles that were done in Arthur's days, until Merlin was lost, as we shall see, through his own foolishness.

On a time Merlin told King Arthur that he should not endure long, but for all his crafts he should be put in the earth alive. Also he told many things that should befall, and how the king would miss him, so that rather than all his lands he would wish to have him again.

"Ah," said King Arthur, "since ye know of this, provide against it, and put away by your crafts that misadventure."

"Nay," said Merlin, "it cannot be done." For Merlin, now grown an old man in his dotage, had fallen under the spell of a damsel of the court named Nimue. With her he soon departed from the King, and evermore went with her wheresoever she went. Ofttimes he wished to break away from her, but he was so held that he could not be out of her presence. Ever she made him good cheer, till she had learned from him all she desired of his secret craft, and had made him swear that he would never do any enchantment upon her.

[Illustration: Merlin and Nimue]

They went together over the sea unto the land of Benwick, where Ban was king, that had helped Arthur against his enemies. Here Merlin saw young Launcelot, King Ban's son, and he told the queen that this same child should grow to be a man of great honour, so that all Christendom should speak of his prowess. So the queen was comforted of her great sorrow that she made for the mortal war that King Claudas waged on her lord and on her lands.

The Great Book of Merlin

Then afterwards Nimue and Merlin departed into Cornwall, and by the way he showed her many wonders, and wearied her with his desire for her love. She would fain have been delivered of him, for she was afraid of him, almost believing him a devil's son, and yet she could not put him away by any means.

And so on a time it happened that Merlin showed to her a wonderful cavern in the cliff, closed by an enchanted stone. By her subtle working she soon made Merlin remove the stone and go into the cavern to let her know of the marvels there. Then she so wrought through the magic he had taught her that the stone was placed back again, so that he never came out for all the craft that he could do. And then she departed and left him there.

On a day a certain knight rode to see adventures, and happened to come to the rock where Nimue had put Merlin, and there he heard him make great lamentation. The knight would gladly have helped him, and tried to move the great stone; but it was so heavy that a hundred men might not lift it up. When Merlin knew that the knight sought his deliverance, he bade him leave his labour, for all was in vain. He could never be helped but by her that put him there.

So Merlin's prophecy of his own end was fulfilled, and he passed from the world of men. Arthur truly missed his old friend and marvelled what had become of him. Afterwards, when the last great battle came, he would have given everything to have Merlin with him again, but it could not be.

Merlin I

Thy trivial harp will never please
Or fill my craving ear;
Its chords should ring as blows the breeze,
Free, peremptory, clear.
No jingling serenader's art,
Nor tinkle of piano strings,
Can make the wild blood start
In its mystic springs.
The kingly bard
Must smite the chords rudely and hard,
As with hammer or with mace;
That they may render back
Artful thunder, which conveys
Secrets of the solar track,
Sparks of the supersolar blaze.

Merlin's blows are strokes of fate,
Chiming with the forest tone,
When boughs buffet boughs in the wood;
Chiming with the gasp and moan
Of the ice-imprisoned flood;
With the pulse of manly hearts;
With the voice or orators;
With the din of city arts;
With the cannonade of wars;
With the marches of the brave;
And prayers of might from martyrs' cave.

Great is the art,
Great be the manners, of the bard.
He shall not his brain encumber
With the coil of rhythm and number;
But, leaving rule and pale forethought,
He shall aye climb
For his rhyme.
"Pass in, pass in," the angels say,
"In to the upper doors,

Nor count compartments of the floors,
But mount to paradise
By the stairway of surprise."

Blameless master of the games,
King of sport that never shames,
He shall daily joy dispense
Hid in song's sweet influence.
Forms more cheerly live and go,
What time the subtle mind
Sings aloud the tune whereto
Their pulses beat,
And march their feet,
And their members are combined.

By Sybarites beguiled,
He shall no task decline;
Merlin's mighty line
Extremes of nature reconciled, –
Bereaved a tyrant of his will,
And made the lion mild.
Songs can the tempest still,
Scattered on the stormy air,
Mold the year to fair increase,
And bring in poetic peace.
He shall not seek to weave,
In weak, unhappy times,
Efficacious rhymes;
Wait his returning strength.
Bird that from the nadir's floor
To the zenith's top can soar, –
The soaring orbit of the muse exceeds that journey's length.
Nor profane affect to hit
Or compass that, by meddling wit,
Which only the propitious mind
Publishes when 'tis inclined.
There are open hours
When the God's will sallies free,

And the dull idiot might see
The flowing fortunes of a thousand years; –
Sudden, at unawares,
Self-moved, fly-to the doors,
Nor sword of angels could reveal
What they conceal.

The Story of Merlin

Here followeth a particular account of the enchantment of Merlin by a certain damsel, hight Vivien, and of all the circumstances thereunto appertaining.

Likewise it is to be narrated how King Arthur was betrayed by his own sister, and of how he would certainly have been slain only for the help of that same enchantress Vivien who was the cause of Merlin's undoing.

Also it shall be told how the sheath of Excalibur was lost at that time.

Chapter First

How Queen Morgana le Fay Meditated Evil Against King Arthur and How She Sent a Damsel to Beguile the Enchanter, Merlin.

Now Morgana le Fay was a very cunning enchantress, and was so much mistress of magic that she could, by means of potent spells, work her will upon all things, whether quick or dead. For Merlin himself had been her master in times past, and had taught her his arts whilst she was still a young damsel at the Court of Uther-Pendragon. So it was that, next to Merlin, she was, at that time, the most potent enchanter in all the world. Nevertheless she lacked Merlin's foreknowledge of things to happen and his gift of prophecy thereupon, for these things he could not impart unto anyone, wherefore she had not learned them of him.

'Now, after Queen Morgana le Fay had come to the Island of Avalon as aforetold, she brooded a great deal over that affront which she deemed King Arthur had placed upon her house; and the more she brooded upon it the more big did it become in her mind. Wherefore, at last, it seemed to her that she could have no pleasure in life unless she could punish King Arthur for that which he had done. Yea; she would have been glad to see him dead at her feet because of the anger that she felt against him.

'But Queen Morgana was very well aware that she could never do the King, her brother, an injury so long as Merlin was there to safeguard him, for Merlin would certainly foresee any danger that might threaten the King, and would counteract it, wherefore she was aware that if she would destroy the King, she must first destroy Merlin.

'Now, there was at the Court of Queen Morgana le Fay, a certain damsel of such marvellous and bewitching beauty that her like was hardly to be seen in all the world. This damsel was fifteen years old and of royal blood, being the daughter of the King of Northumberland; and her name was

Vivien. This damsel, Vivien, was both wise and cunning beyond all measure for one so young. Moreover, she was without any heart, being cold and cruel to all who were contrary-minded to her wishes. So, because she was so cunning and wise, Queen Morgana liked her and taught her many things of magic and sorcery which she knew. But, notwithstanding all that Queen Morgana did for her, this maiden did not feel any love for her mistress, being altogether devoid of heart.

'One day this damsel and Queen Morgana le Fay sat together in a garden of that magic island of Avalon, and the garden was upon a very high terrace and overlooked the sea. And the day was very fair and the sea so wonderfully blue that it appeared to be as though the blue sky had melted into water and the water into the sky. As Vivien and the Queen sat in this beautiful place, the Queen said to the damsel, "Vivien, what wouldst thou rather have than anything else in all the world?" To which Vivien replied, "Lady, I would rather have such wisdom as thou hast, than anything else."

'Then Queen Morgana laughed and said, "It is possible for thee to be as wise as I am, and wiser too, if so be thou wilt do according to my ordination. For I know a way in which thou mayst obtain wisdom."

'"How may I obtain that wisdom, Lady?" said Vivien.

'Then Queen Morgana le Fay said, "Hearken and I will tell thee. Thou must know that Merlin, whom thou hast several times seen at the Court of King Arthur, is the master of all the wisdom that it is possible for anyone to possess in this world. All that I know of magic Merlin hath taught me, and he knoweth many things that he did not teach me, but which he withheld from me. For Merlin taught me, when I was a young damsel at the Court of my mother's husband, because I was beautiful in his eyes. For Merlin loveth beauty above all things else in the world, and so he taught me many things of magic and was very patient with me.

'"But Merlin hath a gift which belongeth to him and which he cannot communicate to anyone else, for it is instinct with him. That gift is the gift of foreseeing into the future and the power of prophesying thereupon.

'"Yet though he may foresee the fate of others, still he is blind to his own fate. For so he confessed to me several times: that he could not tell what was to happen in his own life when that happening concerned himself alone.

'"Now thou, Vivien, art far more beautiful than I was at thine age. Wherefore I believe that thou wilt easily attract the regard of Merlin unto thee. And if I give thee, besides, a certain charm which I possess, I may cause it to be that Merlin may love thee so much that he will impart to thee a great deal more of his wisdom than ever he taught me when I was his disciple."

'"But thou art to know, Vivien, that in winning this gift of knowledge from Merlin thou wilt put thyself in great peril. For, by and by, when the charm of thy beauty shall have waned with him, then he may easily regret what he hath done in imparting his wisdom to thee; in the which case there will be great danger that he may lay some spell upon thee to deprive thee of thy powers; for it would be impossible that both thou and he could live in the same world and each of ye know so much cunning of magic."

'Now unto all this Vivien listened with a great deal of attention, and when Queen Morgana had ended the damsel said, "Dear Lady, all that thou tellest me is very wonderful, and I find myself possessed with a vehement desire to attain such knowledge in magic as that. Wherefore, if thou wilt help me in this matter so that I may beguile his wisdom from Merlin, thou wilt make of me a debtor unto thee for as long as I may live. And touching the matter of any danger that may fall to me in this affair, I am altogether willing to assume that; for I have a great hope that I may be able to protect myself from Merlin that no harm shall befall me. For when I have drawn all the knowledge that I am able to obtain from him, then I will use that same knowledge to cast such a spell upon him that he shall never be able to harm me or anyone else again. In this I shall play my wit against his wisdom and my beauty against his cunning, and I believe that I shall win at that game."

'Then Queen Morgana fell a-laughing beyond all measure, and when she had stinted her laughter, she cried, "Hey, Vivien! certes thou art cunning beyond anything that I ever heard tell of, and I believe that thou art as wicked as thou art cunning. For whoever heard of a child of fifteen years old who would speak such words as thou hast just now spoken; or whoever could suppose that so young a girl could conceive the thought of compassing the downfall of the wisest magician who hath ever lived."

'Then Queen Morgana le Fay set to her lips a small whistle of ivory and gold and blew very shrilly upon it, and in reply there came running a young page of her Court. Queen Morgana commanded him to bring to her a certain casket of alabaster, cunningly carved and adorned with gold and set with several precious stones. And Queen Morgana opened the box and took from within it two rings of pure yellow gold, beautifully wrought and set, the one ring with a clear white stone of extraordinary brilliancy, and the other with a stone as red as blood. Then Queen Morgana said, "Vivien, behold these two rings! They possess each a spell of wonderful potency. For if thou weareth the ring with the white stone, whoever weareth the ring with the red stone shall love thee with such a passion of love that thou mayst do with him whatever thou hast a will to do. So take these rings and go to King Arthur's Court and use them as thy cunning may devise."

'So Vivien took the two rings and gave Queen Morgana le Fay thanks beyond all measure for them.'

'Now King Arthur took much pleasure in holding a great feast each Pentecost, at which time his Court was gathered about him with much mirth and rejoicing. At such times it delighted him to have some excellent entertainment for to amuse himself and his Court, wherefore it befell that nearly always something happened that gave much entertainment to the King. So came the Feast of Pentecost, and King Arthur sat at the table with a great many noble and lordly folk and several kings and queens. Now as they all sat at that feast, their spirits greatly expanded with mirth and good cheer, there suddenly came into the hall a very beautiful young damsel, and with her a dwarf, wonderfully misshapen and of a very hideous countenance. And the maiden was dressed all in flame-colored satin, very rich, and with beautiful embroidery of gold and embroidery of silver. And her hair, which was red like gold, was coiled into a net of gold. And her eyes were black as coals and extraordinarily bright and glistening. And she had about her throat a necklace of gold of three strands, so that with all that gold and those bright garments she shone with wonderful splendor as she entered the hall. Likewise, the dwarf who accompanied her was clad all in flame-colored raiment, and he bore in his hands a cushion of flame-colored silk with tassles of gold, and upon the cushion he bare a ring of exceeding beauty set with a red stone.

'So when King Arthur beheld this beautiful maiden he supposed nothing else, than that there was some excellent entertainment, and at that he rejoiced a very great deal.

'But when he looked well at the damsel it appeared to him that he knew her face, wherefore he said to her, "Damsel, who art thou?" "Sir," she said, "I am the daughter of the King of Northumberland, and my name is Vivien," and thereat King Arthur was satisfied.

'Then King Arthur said to her, "Lady, what is that thou hast upon yonder cushion, and why hast thou honored us by coming hitherward?" To the which Vivien made reply, "Lord, I have here a very good entertainment for to give you pleasure at this Feast of Pentecost. For here is a ring of such a sort that only he who is the most wise and the most worthy of all men here present may wear it." And King Arthur said, "Let us see the ring."

'So Vivien took the ring from the cushion which the dwarf held and she came and brought it unto King Arthur, and the King took the ring into his own hand. And he perceived that the ring was extraordinarily beautiful, wherefore he said, "Maiden, have I thy leave to try this ring upon my finger?" And Vivien said, "Yea, Lord."

'So King Arthur made attempt to place the ring upon his finger; but, lo! the ring shrank in size so that it would not pass beyond the first joint thereof. Wherefore King Arthur said, "It would appear that I am not worthy to wear this ring."

'Then the damsel, Vivien, said, "Have I my lord's leave to offer this ring to others of his Court?" And King Arthur said, "Let the others try the ring." So Vivien took the ring to various folk of the Court, both lords and ladies, but not one of these could wear the ring. Then last of all Vivien came to the place where Merlin sat, and she kneeled upon the ground before him and offered the ring to him; and Merlin, because this concerned himself, could not forecast into the future to know that harm was intended to him. Nevertheless he looked sourly upon the damsel and he said, "Child, what is this silly trick thou offerest me?" "Sir," quoth Vivien, "I beseech you for to try this ring upon your finger." Then Merlin regarded the damsel more closely, and he perceived that she was very beautiful, wherefore his heart softened toward her a great deal. So he spake more gently unto her and he said, "Wherefore should I take the ring?" To the which she made reply, "Because I believe that thou art the most wise and the most worthy of any man in all this place, wherefore the ring should belong to thee."

'Then Merlin smiled, and took the ring and placed it upon his finger, and, lo! it fitted the finger exactly. Thereupon Vivien cried out, "See! the ring hath fitted his finger and he is the most wise and the most worthy." And Merlin was greatly pleased that the ring which the beautiful damsel had given him had fitted his finger in that way.

'Then, after a while, he would have withdrawn the ring again but, behold! he could not, for the ring had grown to his finger as though it were a part of the flesh and bone thereof. At this Merlin became much troubled in spirit and very anxious, for he did not understand what might be meant by the magic of the ring. So he said, "Lady, whence came this ring?" And Vivien said, "Sir, thou knowest all things; dost thou then not know that this ring was sent hitherward from Morgana le Fay?" Then again Merlin was greatly a-doubt, and he said, "I hope there may be no evil in this ring." And Vivien smiled upon him and said, "What evil could there be in it?"

'Now by this time the great magic that was in the ring began to work upon Merlin's spirit, wherefore he regarded Vivien very steadily, and suddenly he took great pleasure in her beauty. Then the magic of the ring gat entire hold upon him and, lo! a wonderful passion immediately seized upon his heart and wrung it so that it was pierced as with a violent agony.

'And Vivien beheld what passed in Merlin's mind, and she laughed and turned away. And several others who were there also observed the very strange manner in which Merlin regarded her, wherefore they said among themselves, "Of a surety Merlin is bewitched by the beauty of that young damoiselle."

'So, after that time the enchantment of the ring of Morgana le Fay so wrought upon Merlin's spirit that he could in no wise disentangle himself from Vivien's witchery; for from that day forth, whithersoever she went, there he might be found not far away; and if she was in the garden, he would be there; and if she was in the Hall, he also would be there; and if she went a-hawking he would also be a-horseback. And all the Court observed these things and many made themselves merry and jested upon it. But, Vivien hated Merlin with all her might, for she saw that they all made merry at that folly of Merlin's, and he wearied her with his regard. But she dissembled this disregard before his face and behaved to him in all ways as though she had a great friendship for him.

'Now it happened upon a day that Vivien sat in the garden, and it was wonderfully pleasant summer weather, and Merlin came into the garden and beheld Vivien where she sat. But when Vivien perceived Merlin coming she suddenly felt so great a disregard for him that she could not bear for to be nigh him at that time, wherefore she arose in haste with intent to escape from him. But Merlin hurried and overtook her and he said to her, "Child, do you then hate me?" And Vivien said, "Sir, I do not hate you." But Merlin said, "In very truth I believe that you do hate me." And Vivien was silent.

'Then in a little Merlin said, "I would that I knew what I might do for you so that you would cease to hate me, for I find that I have a wonderful love for you." Upon this Vivien looked at Merlin very strangely, and by and by she said, "Sir, if you would only impart your wisdom and your cunning unto me, then I believe that I could love you a very great deal. For, behold! I am but as a young child in knowledge and thou art so old and so wise that I am afraid of thee. If thou wouldst teach me thy wisdom so that I might be thine equal, then haply I might grow to have such a regard for thee as thou wouldst have me feel."

'Upon this Merlin looked very steadily at Vivien and he said, "Damsel, thou art, certes, no such foolish child as thou dost proclaim thyself to be; for I see that thine eyes are very bright with a cunning beyond thy years. Now I misdoubt that if I should teach thee the wisdom which thou dost desire to possess, either it would be to thy undoing or else it would be to my undoing."

'Then Vivien cried out with a very loud and piercing voice, "Merlin, if thou dost love me, teach me thy wisdom and the cunning of thy magic and then I will love thee beyond anyone else in all the world!"

'But Merlin sighed very deeply, for his heart misgave him. Then by and by he said, "Vivien, thou shalt have thy will and I will teach thee all those things of wisdom and magic that thou desirest to know."

'Upon this Vivien was filled with such vehement agony of joy that she did not dare to let Merlin look into her countenance lest he should read what was therein written. Wherefore she cast down her eyes and turned her face away from him. Then in a little while she said, "Master, when wilt thou teach me that wisdom?"

'To this Merlin made reply, "I shall not teach thee to-day nor to-morrow nor at this place; for I can only teach thee those knowledges in such solitude that there shall be nothing to disturb thy studies. But to-morrow thou shalt tell King Arthur that thou must return unto thy father's kingdom. Then we will depart together accompanied by thy Court; and when we have come to some secluded place, there I will build a habitation by the means of magic and we shall abide therein until I have instructed thee in wisdom."

'Then Vivien made great joy, and she caught Merlin's hand in hers and she kissed his hand with great passion.

'So the next day Vivien besought King Arthur that he would give her leave to return unto her father's Court, and upon the third day she and Merlin and a number of attendants who were in service upon the damsel, quitted the Court of King Arthur and departed as though to go upon their way to the Kingdom of Northumberland.

'But after they had gone some little distance from the Court of the King, they turned to the eastward and took their way toward a certain valley of which Merlin was acquainted, and which was so fair and pleasant a place that it was sometimes called the Valley of Delight, and sometimes the Valley of Joyousness.

Chapter Second

How Merlin Journeyed With Vivien Unto the Valley of Joyousness and How He Builded for Her a Castle at That Place. Also, How He Taught Her the Wisdom of Magic and of How She Compassed His Downfall Thereby.'

So, Merlin and Vivien and those who were with them travelled for three days to the eastward, until, toward the end of the third day, they reached the confines of a very dark and dismal forest. And there they beheld before them trees so thickly interwoven together that the eyes could not see anything at all of the sky because of the thickness of the foliage. And they beheld the branches and the roots of the trees that they appeared like serpents all twisted together. Wherefore Vivien said, "Sir, this is a very dismal woodland." "Yea," said Merlin, "so it appeareth to be. Ne'theless there lieth within this forest that place which is called by some the Valley of Joyousness, and by others the Valley of Delight, because of the great beauty of that place. And there are several pathways extending through this forest by the means of which that valley may be reached by a man, whether a-horse or afoot."

'And after a while they found it was as Merlin said, for they came by and by upon one of those pathways and entered it and penetrated into the forest. And, lo! within that doleful woodland it was so dark that it appeared as though night-time had fallen, although it was bright daylight beyond the borders thereof, wherefore many of that party were very much afraid. But Merlin ever gave them good cheer and so they went forward upon their way. So, by and by, they came out at last from that place and into the open again, whereat they were greatly rejoiced and took much comfort.

'Now, by this time, the evening had come, very peaceful and tranquil, and they beheld beneath them a valley spread out in that light and it was wonderfully beautiful. And in the centre of the valley was a small lake so smooth and clear, like to crystal, that it appeared like an oval shield of pure silver laid down upon the ground. And all about the margin of the lake were level meadows covered over with an incredible multitude of flowers of divers colors and kinds, very beautiful to behold.

'When Vivien saw this place she cried unto Merlin, "Master, this is, indeed, a very joyous valley, for I do not believe that the blessed meadows of Paradise are more beautiful than this." And Merlin said, "Very well; let us go down into it." So they went down and, as they descended, the night fell apace and the round moon arose in the sky and it was hard to tell whether the valley was the more beautiful in the daytime or whether it was the more beautiful when the moon shone down upon it in that wise.

'So they all came at last unto the borders of the lake and they perceived that there was neither house nor castle at that place.

'Now upon this the followers of Merlin murmured amongst themselves, saying, "This enchanter hath brought us hitherward, but how will he now provide for us that we may find a resting-place that may shelter us from the inclement changes of the weather. For the beauty of this spot cannot alone shelter us from rain and storm." And Merlin overheard their murmurings and he said, "Peace! take ye no trouble upon that matter, for I will very soon provide ye a good resting-place." Then he said to them, "Stand ye a little distance aside till I show ye what I shall do." So they withdrew a little, as he commanded them, and he and Vivien remained where they were. And Vivien said, "Master, what wilt thou do?" And Merlin said, "Wait a little and thou shalt see."

'Therewith he began a certain very powerful conjuration so that the earth began for to tremble and to shake and an appearance as of a great red dust arose into the air. And in this dust there began to appear sundry shapes and forms, and these shapes and forms arose very high into the air and by and by those who gazed thereon perceived that there was a great structure apparent in the midst of the cloud of red dust.

'Then, after a while, all became quiet and the dust slowly disappeared from the air, and, behold! there was the appearance of a marvellous castle such as no one there had ever beheld before, even in a dream. For the walls thereof were of ultramarine and vermilion and they were embellished and adorned with figures of gold, wherefore that castle showed in the moonlight like as it were a pure vision of great glory.

'Now Vivien beheld all that Merlin had accomplished and she went unto him and kneeled down upon the ground before him and took his hand and set it to her lips. And while she kneeled thus, she said, "Master, this is assuredly the most wonderful thing in the world. Wilt thou then teach me such magic that I may be able to build a castle like this castle out of the elements?" And Merlin said, "Yea; all this will I teach thee and more besides; for I will teach thee not only how thou mayst create such a structure as this out of invisible things, but will also teach thee how thou mayst, with a single touch of thy wand, dissipate that castle instantly into the air; even as a child, with a stroke of a straw, may dissipate a beautiful shining bubble, which, upon an instant is, and upon another instant is not. And I will teach thee more than that, for I will teach thee how to change and transform a thing into the semblance of a different thing; and I will teach thee spells and charms such as thou didst never hear tell of before."

'Then Vivien cried out, "Master, thou art the most wonderful man in all of the world!" And Merlin looked upon Vivien and her face was very beautiful in the moonlight and he loved her a very great deal. Wherefore he smiled upon her and said, "Vivien, dost thou still hate me?" And she said, "Nay, master."

'But she spake not the truth, for in her heart she was evil and the heart of Merlin was good, and that which is evil will always hate that which is good. Wherefore, though Vivien lusted for the knowledge of necromancy, and though she spake so lovingly with her lips, yet in her spirit she both feared and hated Merlin because of his wisdom. For she wist right well that, except for the enchantment of that ring which he wore, Merlin would not love her any longer in that wise. Wherefore she said in her heart, "If Merlin teaches me all of his wisdom, then the world cannot contain both him and me."'

Now Merlin abided with Vivien in that place for a year and a little more, and in that time he taught her all of magic that he was able to impart. So at the end of that time he said unto her, "Vivien, I have now taught thee so much that I believe there is no one in all of the world who knoweth more than thou dost of these things of magic which thou hast studied in this time. For not only hast thou such power of sorcery that thou canst make the invisible elements take form at thy will, and not only canst thou transform at thy will one thing into the appearance of an altogether different thing, but thou hast such potent magic in thy possession that thou mayst entangle any living soul into the meshes thereof, unless that one hath some very good talisman to defend himself from thy wiles. Nor have I myself very much more power than this that I have given to thee."

'So said Merlin, and Vivien was filled with great joy. And she said in her heart, "Now, Merlin, if I have the good fortune to entangle thee in my spells, then shalt thou never behold the world again."

'Now, when the next day had come, Vivien caused a very noble feast to be prepared for herself and Merlin. And by means of the knowledge which Merlin had imparted to her she produced a certain very potent sleeping-potion which was altogether infused into a certain noble wine, and the wine she poured into a golden chalice of extraordinary beauty.

'So when that feast was ended, and whiles she and Merlin sat together, Vivien said, "Master, I have a mind to do thee a great honor." And Merlin said, "What is it?" "Thou shalt see," said Vivien. Therewith she smote her hands together and there immediately came a young page unto where they were, and he bare that chalice and she went to where Merlin sat and kneeled down before him and said, "Sir, I beseech thee to take this chalice and to drink the wine that is within it. For as that wine is both very noble and very precious, so is thy wisdom both very noble and very precious; and as the wine is contained within a chalice of priceless cost, so is thy wisdom contained within a life that hath been beyond all value to the world." Therewith she set her lips to the chalice and kissed the wine that was in it.

'Then Merlin suspected no evil, but he took the chalice and quaffed of the wine with great cheerfulness.

'After that, in a little, the fumes of that potent draught began to arise into the brains of Merlin and it was as though a cloud descended upon his sight, and when this came upon him he was presently aware that he was betrayed, wherefore he cried out thrice in a voice, very bitter and full of agony. "Woe! Woe! Woe!" And then he cried out, "I am betrayed!" And therewith he strove to arise from where he sat but he could not.

'That while Vivien sat with her chin upon her hands and regarded him very steadily, smiling strangely upon him. So presently Merlin ceased his struggles and sank into a sleep so deep that it was almost as though he had gone dead. And when that had happened Vivien arose and leeaned over him and set a very powerful spell upon him. And she stretched out her forefinger and wove an enchantment all about him so that it was as though he was entirely encompassed with a silver web of enchantment. And when she had ended, Merlin could move neither hand nor foot nor even so much as a finger-tip, but was altogether like some great insect that a cunning and beautiful spider had enmeshed in a net-work of fine, strong web.

'Now, when the next morning had come, Merlin awoke from his sleep and he beheld that Vivien sat over against him regarding him very narrowly. And they were in the same room in which he had fallen asleep. And when Vivien perceived that Merlin was awake, she laughed and said, "Merlin, how is it with thee?" And Merlin groaned with great passion, saying, "Vivien, thou hast betrayed me."

'At this Vivien laughed again very shrilly and piercingly, and she said, "Behold! Merlin, thou art altogether in my power; for thou art utterly inwoven in those enchantments which thou, thyself, hast taught me. For lo! thou canst not move a single hair without my will. And when I leave thee, the world shall see thee no more and all thy wisdom shall be my wisdom and all thy power shall be my power, and there shall be no other in the whole world who shall possess the wisdom which I possess."

'Then Merlin groaned with such fervor that it was as though his heart would burst asunder. And he said, "Vivien, thou hast brought me to such shame that even were I released from this spell I could not endure that any man should ever see my face again. For I grieve not for my undoings so much as I grieve at the folly that hath turned mine own wisdom against me to my destruction. So I forgive thee all things that thou hast done to me to betray me; yet there is one thing alone which I crave of thee."

'And Vivien said, "Does it concern thee?" And Merlin said, "No, it concerns another." Thereupon Vivien said, "What is it?"

'Then Merlin said, "It is this: Now I have received my gift of foresight again, and I perceive that King Arthur is presently in great peril of his life. So I beseech thee Vivien that thou wilt straightway go to where he is in danger, and that thou wilt use thy powers of sorcery for to save him. Thus, by fulfilling this one good deed, thou shalt haply lessen the sin of this that thou hast done to betray me."

'Now at that time Vivien was not altogether bad as she afterward became, for she still felt some small pity for Merlin and some small reverence for King Arthur. Wherefore now she laughed and said, "Very well, I will do thy desire in this matter. Whither shall I go to save that King?"

'Then Merlin replied, "Go into the West country and unto the castle of a certain knight hight Sir Domas de Noir, and when thou comest there then thou shalt immediately see how thou mayst be of aid to the good King." Upon this Vivien said, "I will do this thing for thee, for it is the last favor that anyone may ever render unto thee in this world."

'Therewith Vivien smote her hands together and summoned many of her attendants. And when these had come in she presented Merlin before them, and she said, "Behold how I have bewitched him. Go! See for yourselves! Feel of his hands and his face and see if there be any life in him." And they went to Merlin and felt of him; his hands and arms and his face, and even they plucked at his beard, and Merlin could not move in any wise but only groan with great dolor. So they all laughed and made them merry at his woful state.

'Then Vivien caused it by means of her magic that there should be in that place a great coffer of stone. And she commanded those who were there that they should lift Merlin up and lay him therein and they did as she commanded. Then she caused it that, by means of her magic, there should be placed a huge slab of stone upon that coffer such as ten men could hardly lift, and Merlin lay beneath that stone like one who was dead.

'Then Vivien caused it to be that the magic castle should instantly disappear and so it befell as she willed. Then she caused it that a mist should arrive at that place, and the mist was of such sort that no one could penetrate into it, or sever it asunder, nor could any human eye see what was within. Then, when she had done all this, she went her way with all of her Court from that valley, making great joy in that she triumphed over Merlin.

'Nevertheless, she did not forget her promise, but went to the castle of Sir Domas de Noir, and after a while it shall all be told how it befell at that place.'

Such was the passing of Merlin, and God grant it that you may not so misuse the wisdom He giveth you to have, that it may be turned against you to your undoing. For there can be no greater bitterness in the world than this: That a man shall be betrayed by no one to whom he himself hath given the power of betraying him.

'And now turn we unto King Arthur to learn how it fell with him after Merlin had thus been betrayed to his undoing.'

The Egyptian Maid or The Romance of the Water-Lily

While Merlin paced the Cornish sands,
Forth-looking toward the Rocks of Scilly,
The pleased Enchanter was aware
Of a bright Ship that seemed to hang in air,
Yet was she work of mortal hands,
And took from men her name – THE WATER LILY.

Soft was the wind, that landward blew;
And, as the Moon, o'er some dark hill ascendant,
Grows from a little edge of light
To a full orb, this Pinnace bright,
As nearer to the Coast she drew,
Appeared more glorious, with spread sail and pendant.

Upon this winged Shape so fair
Sage Merlin gazed with admiration:
Her lineaments, thought he, surpass
Aught that was ever shown in magic glass;
In patience built with subtle care;
Or, at a touch, set forth with wondrous transformation.

Now, though a Mechanist, whose skill
Shames the degenerate grasp of modern science,
Grave Merlin (and belike the more
For practising occult and perilous lore)
Was subject to a freakish will
That sapped good thoughts, or scared them with defiance.

Provoked to envious spleen, he cast
An altered look upon the advancing Stranger
Whom he had hailed with joy, and cried,
"My Art shall help to tame her pride – "
Anon the breeze became a blast,
And the waves rose, and sky portended danger.

With thrilling word, and potent sign

The Great Book of Merlin

Traced on the beach, his work the Sorcerer urges;
The clouds in blacker clouds are lost,
Like spiteful Fiends that vanish, crossed
By Fiends of aspect more malign;
And the winds roused the Deep with fiercer scourges.

But worthy of the name she bore
Was this Sea-flower, this buoyant Galley;
Supreme in loveliness and grace
Of motion, whether in the embrace
Of trusty anchorage, or scudding o'er
The main flood roughened into hill and valley.

Behold, how wantonly she laves
Her sides, the Wizard's craft confounding;
Like something out of Ocean sprung
To be for ever fresh and young,
Breasts the sea-flashes, and huge waves
Top-gallant high, rebounding and rebounding!

But Ocean under magic heaves,
And cannot spare the Thing he cherished:
Ah! what avails that She was fair,
Luminous, blithe, and debonair?
The storm has stripped her of her leaves;
The Lily floats no longer! – She hath perished.

Grieve for her, – She deserves no less;
So like, yet so unlike, a living Creature!
No heart had she, no busy brain;
Though loved, she could not love again;
Though pitied, feel her own distress;
Nor aught that troubles us, the fools of Nature.

Yet is there cause for gushing tears;
So richly was this Galley laden;
A fairer than Herself she bore,
And, in her struggles, cast ashore;

A Book of Merlin

A lovely One, who nothing hears
Of wind or wave – a meek and guileless Maiden.

Into a cave had Merlin fled
From mischief, caused by spells himself had muttered;
And, while repentant all too late,
In moody posture there he sate,
He heard a voice, and saw, with half-raised head,
A Visitant by whom these words were uttered:

"On Christian service this frail Bark
Sailed" (hear me, Merlin!) "under high protection,
Though on her prow a sign of heathen power
Was carved – a Goddess with a Lily flower,
The old Egyptian's emblematic mark
Of joy immortal and of pure affection.

"Her course was for the British strand,
Her freight it was a Damsel peerless;
God reigns above, and Spirits strong
May gather to avenge this wrong
Done to the Princess, and her Land
Which she in duty left, though sad not cheerless.

"And to Caerleon's loftiest tower
Soon will the Knights of Arthur's Table
A cry of lamentation send;
And all will weep who there attend,
To grace that Stranger's bridal hour,
For whom the sea was made unnavigable.

"Shame! should a Child of Royal Line
Die through the blindness of thy malice:"
Thus to the Necromancer spake
Nina, the Lady of the Lake,
A gentle Sorceress, and benign,
Who ne'er embittered any good man's chalice.

The Great Book of Merlin

"What boots," continued she, "to mourn?
To expiate thy sin endeavour!
From the bleak isle where she is laid,
Fetched by our art, the Egyptian Maid
May yet to Arthur's court be borne
Cold as she is, ere life be fled for ever.

"My pearly Boat, a shining Light,
That brought me down that sunless river,
Will bear me on from wave to wave,
And back with her to this sea-cave;
Then Merlin! for a rapid flight
Through air to thee my charge will I deliver.

"The very swiftest of thy Cars
Must, when my part is done, be ready;
Meanwhile, for further guidance, look
Into thy own prophetic book;
And, if that fail, consult the Stars
To learn thy course; farewell! be prompt and steady."

This scarcely spoken, she again
Was seated in her gleaming Shallop,
That, o'er the yet-distempered Deep,
Pursued its way with bird-like sweep,
Or like a steed, without a rein,
Urged o'er the wilderness in sportive gallop.

Soon did the gentle Nina reach
That Isle without a house or haven;
Landing, she found not what she sought,
Nor saw of wreck or ruin aught
But a carved Lotus cast upon the shore
By the fierce waves, a flower in marble graven.

Sad relique, but how fair the while!
For gently each from each retreating
With backward curve, the leaves revealed

The bosom half, and half concealed,
Of a Divinity, that seemed to smile
On Nina as she passed, with hopeful greeting.

No quest was hers of vague desire,
Of tortured hope and purpose shaken;
Following the margin of a bay,
She spied the lonely Cast-away,
Unmarred, unstripped of her attire,
But with closed eyes, – of breath and bloom forsaken.

Then Nina, stooping down, embraced,
With tenderness and mild emotion,
The Damsel, in that trance embound;
And, while she raised her from the ground,
And in the pearly shallop placed,
Sleep fell upon the air, and stilled the ocean.

The turmoil hushed, celestial springs
Of music opened, and there came a blending
Of fragrance, underived from earth,
With gleams that owed not to the Sun their birth,
And that soft rustling of invisible wings
Which Angels make, on works of love descending.

And Nina heard a sweeter voice
Than if the Goddess of the Flower had spoken:
"Thou hast achieved, fair Dame! what none
Less pure in spirit could have done;
Go, in thy enterprise rejoice!
Air, earth, sea, sky, and heaven, success betoken."

So cheered she left that Island bleak,
A bare rock of the Scilly cluster;
And, as they traversed the smooth brine,
The self-illumined Brigantine
Shed, on the Slumberer's cold wan cheek
And pallid brow, a melancholy lustre.

The Great Book of Merlin

Fleet was their course, and when they came
To the dim cavern, whence the river
Issued into the salt-sea flood,
Merlin, as fixed in thought he stood,
Was thus accosted by the Dame:
"Behold to thee my Charge I now deliver!

"But where attends thy chariot – where?"
Quoth Merlin, "Even as I was bidden,
So have I done; as trusty as thy barge
My vehicle shall prove – O precious Charge!
If this be sleep, how soft! if death, how fair!
Much have my books disclosed, but the end is hidden."

He spake, and gliding into view
Forth from the grotto's dimmest chamber
Came two mute Swans, whose plumes of dusky white
Changed, as the pair approached the light,
Drawing an ebon car, their hue
(Like clouds of sunset) into lucid amber.

Once more did gentle Nina lift
The Princess, passive to all changes:
The car received her; then up-went
Into the ethereal element
The Birds with progress smooth and swift
As thought, when through bright regions memory ranges.

Sage Merlin, at the Slumberer's side,
Instructs the Swans their way to measure;
And soon Caerleon's towers appeared,
And notes of minstrelsy were heard
From rich pavilions spreading wide,
For some high day of long-expected pleasure.

Awe-stricken stood both Knights and Dames
Ere on firm ground the car alighted;
Eftsoons astonishment was past,

A Book of Merlin

For in that face they saw the last
Last lingering look of clay, that tames
All pride, by which all happiness is blighted.

Said Merlin, "Mighty King, fair Lords,
Away with feast and tilt and tourney!
Ye saw, throughout this Royal House,
Ye heard, a rocking marvellous
Of turrets, and a clash of swords
Self-shaken, as I closed my airy journey.

"Lo! by a destiny well known
To mortals, joy is turned to sorrow;
This is the wished-for Bride, the Maid
Of Egypt, from a rock conveyed
Where she by shipwreck had been thrown;
Ill sight! but grief may vanish ere the morrow."

"Though vast thy power, thy words are weak,"
Exclaimed the King, "a mockery hateful;
Dutiful Child! her lot how hard!
Is this her piety's reward?
Those watery locks, that bloodless cheek!
O winds without remorse!   O shore ungrateful!

"Rich robes are fretted by the moth;
Towers, temples, fall by stroke of thunder;
Will that, or deeper thoughts, abate
A Father's sorrow for her fate?
He will repent him of his troth;
His brain will burn, his stout heart split asunder.

"Alas! and I have caused this woe;
For, when my prowess from invading Neighbours
Had freed his Realm, he plighted word
That he would turn to Christ our Lord,
And his dear Daughter on a Knight bestow
Whom I should choose for love and matchless labours.

"Her birth was heathen, but a fence
Of holy Angels round her hovered;
A Lady added to my court
So fair, of such divine report
And worship, seemed a recompence
For fifty kingdoms by my sword recovered.

"Ask not for whom, O champions true!
She was reserved by me her life's betrayer;
She who was meant to be a bride
Is now a corse; then put aside
Vain thoughts, and speed ye, with observance due
Of Christian rites, in Christian ground to lay her."

"The tomb," said Merlin, "may not close
Upon her yet, earth hide her beauty;
Not froward to thy sovereign will
Esteem me, Liege! if I, whose skill
Wafted her hither, interpose
To check this pious haste of erring duty.

"My books command me to lay bare
The secret thou art bent on keeping;
Here must a high attest be given,
What Bridegroom was for her ordained by Heaven;
And in my glass significants there are
Of things that may to gladness turn this weeping.

"For this, approaching, One by One,
Thy Knights must touch the cold hand of the Virgin;
So, for the favoured One, the Flower may bloom
Once more; but, if unchangeagble her doom,
If life departed be for ever gone,
Some blest assurance, from this cloud emerging,

May teach him to bewail his loss;
Not with a grief that, like a vapour, rises
And melts; but grief devout that shall endure

A Book of Merlin

And a perpetual growth secure
Of purposes which no false thought shall cross
A harvest of high hopes and noble enterprises."

"So be it," said the King; – "anon,
Here, where the Princess lies, begin the trial;
Knights each in order as ye stand
Step forth." – To touch the pallid hand
Sir Agravaine advanced; no sign he won
From Heaven or Earth; – Sir Kaye had like denial.

Abashed, Sir Dinas turned away;
Even for Sir Percival was no disclosure;
Though he, devoutest of all Champions, ere
He reached that ebon car, the bier
Whereon diffused like snow the Damsel lay,
Full thrice had crossed himself in meek composure.

Imagine (but ye Saints! who can?)
How in still air the balance trembled;
The wishes, peradventure the despites
That overcame some not ungenerous Knights;
And all the thoughts that lengthened out a span
Of time to Lords and Ladies thus assembled.

What patient confidence was here!
And there how many bosoms panted!
While drawing toward the Car Sir Gawaine, mailed
For tournament, his Beaver vailed,
And softly touched; but, to his princely cheer
And high expectancy, no sign was granted.

Next, disencumbered of his harp,
Sir Tristram, dear to thousands as a brother,
Came to the proof, nor grieved that there ensued
No change; – the fair Izonda he had wooed
With love too true, a love with pangs too sharp,
From hope too distant, not to dread another.

81

The Great Book of Merlin

Not so Sir Launcelot; – from Heaven's grace
A sign he craved, tired slave of vain contrition;
The royal Guinever looked passing glad
When his touch failed. – Next came Sir Galahad;
He paused, and stood entranced by that still face
Whose features he had seen in noontide vision.

For late, as near a murmuring stream
He rested 'mid an arbour green and shady,
Nina, the good Enchantress, shed
A light around his mossy bed;
And, at her call, a waking dream
Prefigured to his sense the Egyptian Lady.

Now, while the bright-haired front he bowed,
And stood, far-kenned by mantle furred with ermine,
As o'er the insensate Body hung
The enrapt, the beautiful, the young,
Belief sank deep into the crowd
That he the solemn issue would determine.

Nor deem it strange; the Youth had worn
That very mantle on a day of glory,
The day when he achieved that matchless feat,
The marvel of the PERILOUS SEAT,
Which whosoe'er approached of strength was shorn,
Though King or Knight the most renowned in story.

He touched with hesitating hand,
And lo! those Birds, far-famed through Love's dominions,
The Swans, in triumph clap their wings;
And their necks play, involved in rings,
Like sinless snakes in Eden's happy land; –
"Mine is she," cried the Knight; – again they clapped their pinions.

"Mine was she – mine she is, though dead,
And to her name my soul shall cleave in sorrow;"
Whereat, a tender twilight streak

Of colour dawned upon the Damsel's cheek;
And her lips, quickening with uncertain red,
Seemed from each other a faint warmth to borrow.

Deep was the awe, the rapture high,
Of love emboldened, hope with dread entwining,
When, to the mouth, relenting Death
Allowed a soft and flower-like breath,
Precursor to a timid sigh,
To lifted eyelids, and a doubtful shining.

In silence did King Arthur gaze
Upon the signs that pass away or tarry;
In silence watched the gentle strife
Of Nature leading back to life;
Then eased his Soul at length by praise
Of God, and Heaven's pure Queen – the blissful Mary.

Then said he, "Take her to thy heart
Sir Galahad! a treasure that God giveth
Bound by indissoluble ties to thee
Through mortal change and immortality;
Be happy and unenvied, thou who art
A goodly Knight that hath no Peer that liveth!"

Not long the Nuptials were delayed;
And sage tradition still rehearses
The pomp the glory of that hour
When toward the Altar from her bower
King Arthur led the Egyptian Maid,
And Angels carolled these far-echoed verses; –

Who shrinks not from alliance
Of evil with good Powers,
To God proclaims defiance,
And mocks whom he adores.

A Ship to Christ devoted

The Great Book of Merlin

From the Land of Nile did go;
Alas! the bright Ship floated,
An Idol at her Prow.

By magic domination
The Heaven-permitted vent
Of purblind mortal passion,
Was wrought her punishment.

The Flower, the Form within it,
What served they in her need?
Her port she could not win it,
Nor from mishap be freed.

The tempest overcame her,
And she was seen no more;
But gently gently blame her,
She cast a Pearl ashore.

The Maid to Jesu hearkened,
And kept to him her faith,
Till sense in death was darkened,
Or sleep akin to death.

But Angels round her pillow
Kept watch, a viewless band;
And, billow favouring billow,
She reached the destined strand.

Blest Pair! whate'er befall you,
Your faith in Him approve
Who from frail earth can call you,
To bowers of endless love!

Merlin and Vivien

A storm was coming, but the winds were still,
And in the wild woods of Broceliande,
Before an oak, so hollow, huge and old
It looked a tower of ivied masonwork,
At Merlin's feet the wily Vivien lay.

For he that always bare in bitter grudge
The slights of Arthur and his Table, Mark
The Cornish King, had heard a wandering voice,
A minstrel of Caerlon by strong storm
Blown into shelter at Tintagil, say
That out of naked knightlike purity
Sir Lancelot worshipt no unmarried girl
But the great Queen herself, fought in her name,
Sware by her—vows like theirs, that high in heaven
Love most, but neither marry, nor are given
In marriage, angels of our Lord's report.

He ceased, and then—for Vivien sweetly said
(She sat beside the banquet nearest Mark),
'And is the fair example followed, Sir,
In Arthur's household?'—answered innocently:

'Ay, by some few—ay, truly—youths that hold
It more beseems the perfect virgin knight
To worship woman as true wife beyond
All hopes of gaining, than as maiden girl.
They place their pride in Lancelot and the Queen.
So passionate for an utter purity
Beyond the limit of their bond, are these,
For Arthur bound them not to singleness.
Brave hearts and clean! and yet—God guide them—young.'

Then Mark was half in heart to hurl his cup
Straight at the speaker, but forbore: he rose
To leave the hall, and, Vivien following him,
Turned to her: 'Here are snakes within the grass;
And you methinks, O Vivien, save ye fear
The monkish manhood, and the mask of pure
Worn by this court, can stir them till they sting.'

And Vivien answered, smiling scornfully,
'Why fear? because that fostered at THY court
I savour of thy—virtues? fear them? no.
As Love, if Love is perfect, casts out fear,
So Hate, if Hate is perfect, casts out fear.
My father died in battle against the King,
My mother on his corpse in open field;
She bore me there, for born from death was I
Among the dead and sown upon the wind—
And then on thee! and shown the truth betimes,
That old true filth, and bottom of the well
Where Truth is hidden. Gracious lessons thine
And maxims of the mud! "This Arthur pure!
Great Nature through the flesh herself hath made
Gives him the lie! There is no being pure,
My cherub; saith not Holy Writ the same?"—
If I were Arthur, I would have thy blood.
Thy blessing, stainless King! I bring thee back,
When I have ferreted out their burrowings,
The hearts of all this Order in mine hand—
Ay—so that fate and craft and folly close,
Perchance, one curl of Arthur's golden beard.
To me this narrow grizzled fork of thine
Is cleaner-fashioned—Well, I loved thee first,
That warps the wit.'

Loud laughed the graceless Mark,
But Vivien, into Camelot stealing, lodged
Low in the city, and on a festal day
When Guinevere was crossing the great hall
Cast herself down, knelt to the Queen, and wailed.

'Why kneel ye there? What evil hath ye wrought?
Rise!' and the damsel bidden rise arose
And stood with folded hands and downward eyes
Of glancing corner, and all meekly said,
'None wrought, but suffered much, an orphan maid!
My father died in battle for thy King,
My mother on his corpse—in open field,
The sad sea-sounding wastes of Lyonnesse—
Poor wretch—no friend!—and now by Mark the King

A Book of Merlin

For that small charm of feature mine, pursued—
If any such be mine—I fly to thee.
Save, save me thou—Woman of women—thine
The wreath of beauty, thine the crown of power,
Be thine the balm of pity, O Heaven's own white
Earth-angel, stainless bride of stainless King—
Help, for he follows! take me to thyself!
O yield me shelter for mine innocency
Among thy maidens!

Here her slow sweet eyes
Fear-tremulous, but humbly hopeful, rose
Fixt on her hearer's, while the Queen who stood
All glittering like May sunshine on May leaves
In green and gold, and plumed with green replied,
'Peace, child! of overpraise and overblame
We choose the last. Our noble Arthur, him
Ye scarce can overpraise, will hear and know.
Nay—we believe all evil of thy Mark—
Well, we shall test thee farther; but this hour
We ride a-hawking with Sir Lancelot.
He hath given us a fair falcon which he trained;
We go to prove it. Bide ye here the while.'

She past; and Vivien murmured after 'Go!
I bide the while.' Then through the portal-arch
Peering askance, and muttering broken-wise,
As one that labours with an evil dream,
Beheld the Queen and Lancelot get to horse.

'Is that the Lancelot? goodly—ay, but gaunt:
Courteous—amends for gauntness—takes her hand—
That glance of theirs, but for the street, had been
A clinging kiss—how hand lingers in hand!
Let go at last!—they ride away—to hawk
For waterfowl. Royaller game is mine.
For such a supersensual sensual bond
As that gray cricket chirpt of at our hearth—
Touch flax with flame—a glance will serve—the liars!
Ah little rat that borest in the dyke
Thy hole by night to let the boundless deep

Down upon far-off cities while they dance—
Or dream—of thee they dreamed not—nor of me
These—ay, but each of either: ride, and dream
The mortal dream that never yet was mine—
Ride, ride and dream until ye wake—to me!
Then, narrow court and lubber King, farewell!
For Lancelot will be gracious to the rat,
And our wise Queen, if knowing that I know,
Will hate, loathe, fear—but honour me the more.'

Yet while they rode together down the plain,
Their talk was all of training, terms of art,
Diet and seeling, jesses, leash and lure.
'She is too noble' he said 'to check at pies,
Nor will she rake: there is no baseness in her.'
Here when the Queen demanded as by chance
'Know ye the stranger woman?' 'Let her be,'
Said Lancelot and unhooded casting off
The goodly falcon free; she towered; her bells,
Tone under tone, shrilled; and they lifted up
Their eager faces, wondering at the strength,
Boldness and royal knighthood of the bird
Who pounced her quarry and slew it. Many a time
As once—of old—among the flowers—they rode.

But Vivien half-forgotten of the Queen
Among her damsels broidering sat, heard, watched
And whispered: through the peaceful court she crept
And whispered: then as Arthur in the highest
Leavened the world, so Vivien in the lowest,
Arriving at a time of golden rest,
And sowing one ill hint from ear to ear,
While all the heathen lay at Arthur's feet,
And no quest came, but all was joust and play,
Leavened his hall. They heard and let her be.

Thereafter as an enemy that has left
Death in the living waters, and withdrawn,
The wily Vivien stole from Arthur's court.

She hated all the knights, and heard in thought

Their lavish comment when her name was named.
For once, when Arthur walking all alone,
Vext at a rumour issued from herself
Of some corruption crept among his knights,
Had met her, Vivien, being greeted fair,
Would fain have wrought upon his cloudy mood
With reverent eyes mock-loyal, shaken voice,
And fluttered adoration, and at last
With dark sweet hints of some who prized him more
Than who should prize him most; at which the King
Had gazed upon her blankly and gone by:
But one had watched, and had not held his peace:
It made the laughter of an afternoon
That Vivien should attempt the blameless King.
And after that, she set herself to gain
Him, the most famous man of all those times,
Merlin, who knew the range of all their arts,
Had built the King his havens, ships, and halls,
Was also Bard, and knew the starry heavens;
The people called him Wizard; whom at first
She played about with slight and sprightly talk,
And vivid smiles, and faintly-venomed points
Of slander, glancing here and grazing there;
And yielding to his kindlier moods, the Seer
Would watch her at her petulance, and play,
Even when they seemed unloveable, and laugh
As those that watch a kitten; thus he grew
Tolerant of what he half disdained, and she,
Perceiving that she was but half disdained,
Began to break her sports with graver fits,
Turn red or pale, would often when they met
Sigh fully, or all-silent gaze upon him
With such a fixt devotion, that the old man,
Though doubtful, felt the flattery, and at times
Would flatter his own wish in age for love,
And half believe her true: for thus at times
He wavered; but that other clung to him,
Fixt in her will, and so the seasons went.

Then fell on Merlin a great melancholy;
He walked with dreams and darkness, and he found

The Great Book of Merlin

A doom that ever poised itself to fall,
An ever-moaning battle in the mist,
World-war of dying flesh against the life,
Death in all life and lying in all love,
The meanest having power upon the highest,
And the high purpose broken by the worm.

So leaving Arthur's court he gained the beach;
There found a little boat, and stept into it;
And Vivien followed, but he marked her not.
She took the helm and he the sail; the boat
Drave with a sudden wind across the deeps,
And touching Breton sands, they disembarked.
And then she followed Merlin all the way,
Even to the wild woods of Broceliande.
For Merlin once had told her of a charm,
The which if any wrought on anyone
With woven paces and with waving arms,
The man so wrought on ever seemed to lie
Closed in the four walls of a hollow tower,
From which was no escape for evermore;
And none could find that man for evermore,
Nor could he see but him who wrought the charm
Coming and going, and he lay as dead
And lost to life and use and name and fame.
And Vivien ever sought to work the charm
Upon the great Enchanter of the Time,
As fancying that her glory would be great
According to his greatness whom she quenched.

There lay she all her length and kissed his feet,
As if in deepest reverence and in love.
A twist of gold was round her hair; a robe
Of samite without price, that more exprest
Than hid her, clung about her lissome limbs,
In colour like the satin-shining palm
On sallows in the windy gleams of March:
And while she kissed them, crying, 'Trample me,
Dear feet, that I have followed through the world,
And I will pay you worship; tread me down
And I will kiss you for it;' he was mute:

A Book of Merlin

So dark a forethought rolled about his brain,
As on a dull day in an Ocean cave
The blind wave feeling round his long sea-hall
In silence: wherefore, when she lifted up
A face of sad appeal, and spake and said,
'O Merlin, do ye love me?' and again,
'O Merlin, do ye love me?' and once more,
'Great Master, do ye love me?' he was mute.
And lissome Vivien, holding by his heel,
Writhed toward him, slided up his knee and sat,
Behind his ankle twined her hollow feet
Together, curved an arm about his neck,
Clung like a snake; and letting her left hand
Droop from his mighty shoulder, as a leaf,
Made with her right a comb of pearl to part
The lists of such a board as youth gone out
Had left in ashes: then he spoke and said,
Not looking at her, 'Who are wise in love
Love most, say least,' and Vivien answered quick,
'I saw the little elf-god eyeless once
In Arthur's arras hall at Camelot:
But neither eyes nor tongue—O stupid child!
Yet you are wise who say it; let me think
Silence is wisdom: I am silent then,
And ask no kiss;' then adding all at once,
'And lo, I clothe myself with wisdom,' drew
The vast and shaggy mantle of his beard
Across her neck and bosom to her knee,
And called herself a gilded summer fly
Caught in a great old tyrant spider's web,
Who meant to eat her up in that wild wood
Without one word. So Vivien called herself,
But rather seemed a lovely baleful star
Veiled in gray vapour; till he sadly smiled:
'To what request for what strange boon,' he said,
'Are these your pretty tricks and fooleries,
O Vivien, the preamble? yet my thanks,
For these have broken up my melancholy.'

And Vivien answered smiling saucily,
'What, O my Master, have ye found your voice?

The Great Book of Merlin

I bid the stranger welcome. Thanks at last!
But yesterday you never opened lip,
Except indeed to drink: no cup had we:
In mine own lady palms I culled the spring
That gathered trickling dropwise from the cleft,
And made a pretty cup of both my hands
And offered you it kneeling: then you drank
And knew no more, nor gave me one poor word;
O no more thanks than might a goat have given
With no more sign of reverence than a beard.
And when we halted at that other well,
And I was faint to swooning, and you lay
Foot-gilt with all the blossom-dust of those
Deep meadows we had traversed, did you know
That Vivien bathed your feet before her own?
And yet no thanks: and all through this wild wood
And all this morning when I fondled you:
Boon, ay, there was a boon, one not so strange—
How had I wronged you? surely ye are wise,
But such a silence is more wise than kind.'

And Merlin locked his hand in hers and said:
'O did ye never lie upon the shore,
And watch the curled white of the coming wave
Glassed in the slippery sand before it breaks?
Even such a wave, but not so pleasurable,
Dark in the glass of some presageful mood,
Had I for three days seen, ready to fall.
And then I rose and fled from Arthur's court
To break the mood. You followed me unasked;
And when I looked, and saw you following me still,
My mind involved yourself the nearest thing
In that mind-mist: for shall I tell you truth?
You seemed that wave about to break upon me
And sweep me from my hold upon the world,
My use and name and fame. Your pardon, child.
Your pretty sports have brightened all again.
And ask your boon, for boon I owe you thrice,
Once for wrong done you by confusion, next
For thanks it seems till now neglected, last
For these your dainty gambols: wherefore ask;

A Book of Merlin

And take this boon so strange and not so strange.'

And Vivien answered smiling mournfully:
'O not so strange as my long asking it,
Not yet so strange as you yourself are strange,
Nor half so strange as that dark mood of yours.
I ever feared ye were not wholly mine;
And see, yourself have owned ye did me wrong.
The people call you prophet: let it be:
But not of those that can expound themselves.
Take Vivien for expounder; she will call
That three-days-long presageful gloom of yours
No presage, but the same mistrustful mood
That makes you seem less noble than yourself,
Whenever I have asked this very boon,
Now asked again: for see you not, dear love,
That such a mood as that, which lately gloomed
Your fancy when ye saw me following you,
Must make me fear still more you are not mine,
Must make me yearn still more to prove you mine,
And make me wish still more to learn this charm
Of woven paces and of waving hands,
As proof of trust. O Merlin, teach it me.
The charm so taught will charm us both to rest.
For, grant me some slight power upon your fate,
I, feeling that you felt me worthy trust,
Should rest and let you rest, knowing you mine.
And therefore be as great as ye are named,
Not muffled round with selfish reticence.
How hard you look and how denyingly!
O, if you think this wickedness in me,
That I should prove it on you unawares,
That makes me passing wrathful; then our bond
Had best be loosed for ever: but think or not,
By Heaven that hears I tell you the clean truth,
As clean as blood of babes, as white as milk:
O Merlin, may this earth, if ever I,
If these unwitty wandering wits of mine,
Even in the jumbled rubbish of a dream,
Have tript on such conjectural treachery—
May this hard earth cleave to the Nadir hell

Down, down, and close again, and nip me flat,
If I be such a traitress. Yield my boon,
Till which I scarce can yield you all I am;
And grant my re-reiterated wish,
The great proof of your love: because I think,
However wise, ye hardly know me yet.'

And Merlin loosed his hand from hers and said,
'I never was less wise, however wise,
Too curious Vivien, though you talk of trust,
Than when I told you first of such a charm.
Yea, if ye talk of trust I tell you this,
Too much I trusted when I told you that,
And stirred this vice in you which ruined man
Through woman the first hour; for howsoe'er
In children a great curiousness be well,
Who have to learn themselves and all the world,
In you, that are no child, for still I find
Your face is practised when I spell the lines,
I call it,—well, I will not call it vice:
But since you name yourself the summer fly,
I well could wish a cobweb for the gnat,
That settles, beaten back, and beaten back
Settles, till one could yield for weariness:
But since I will not yield to give you power
Upon my life and use and name and fame,
Why will ye never ask some other boon?
Yea, by God's rood, I trusted you too much.'

And Vivien, like the tenderest-hearted maid
That ever bided tryst at village stile,
Made answer, either eyelid wet with tears:
'Nay, Master, be not wrathful with your maid;
Caress her: let her feel herself forgiven
Who feels no heart to ask another boon.
I think ye hardly know the tender rhyme
Of "trust me not at all or all in all."
I heard the great Sir Lancelot sing it once,
And it shall answer for me. Listen to it.

"In Love, if Love be Love, if Love be ours,

Faith and unfaith can ne'er be equal powers:
Unfaith in aught is want of faith in all.

"It is the little rift within the lute,
That by and by will make the music mute,
And ever widening slowly silence all.

"The little rift within the lover's lute
Or little pitted speck in garnered fruit,
That rotting inward slowly moulders all.

"It is not worth the keeping: let it go:
But shall it? answer, darling, answer, no.
And trust me not at all or all in all."

O Master, do ye love my tender rhyme?'

And Merlin looked and half believed her true,
So tender was her voice, so fair her face,
So sweetly gleamed her eyes behind her tears
Like sunlight on the plain behind a shower:
And yet he answered half indignantly:

'Far other was the song that once I heard
By this huge oak, sung nearly where we sit:
For here we met, some ten or twelve of us,
To chase a creature that was current then
In these wild woods, the hart with golden horns.
It was the time when first the question rose
About the founding of a Table Round,
That was to be, for love of God and men
And noble deeds, the flower of all the world.
And each incited each to noble deeds.
And while we waited, one, the youngest of us,
We could not keep him silent, out he flashed,
And into such a song, such fire for fame,
Such trumpet-glowings in it, coming down
To such a stern and iron-clashing close,
That when he stopt we longed to hurl together,
And should have done it; but the beauteous beast
Scared by the noise upstarted at our feet,

The Great Book of Merlin

And like a silver shadow slipt away
Through the dim land; and all day long we rode
Through the dim land against a rushing wind,
That glorious roundel echoing in our ears,
And chased the flashes of his golden horns
Till they vanished by the fairy well
That laughs at iron—as our warriors did—
Where children cast their pins and nails, and cry,
"Laugh, little well!" but touch it with a sword,
It buzzes fiercely round the point; and there
We lost him: such a noble song was that.
But, Vivien, when you sang me that sweet rhyme,
I felt as though you knew this cursd charm,
Were proving it on me, and that I lay
And felt them slowly ebbing, name and fame.'

And Vivien answered smiling mournfully:
'O mine have ebbed away for evermore,
And all through following you to this wild wood,
Because I saw you sad, to comfort you.
Lo now, what hearts have men! they never mount
As high as woman in her selfless mood.
And touching fame, howe'er ye scorn my song,
Take one verse more—the lady speaks it—this:

'"My name, once mine, now thine, is closelier mine,
For fame, could fame be mine, that fame were thine,
And shame, could shame be thine, that shame were mine.
So trust me not at all or all in all."

'Says she not well? and there is more—this rhyme
Is like the fair pearl-necklace of the Queen,
That burst in dancing, and the pearls were spilt;
Some lost, some stolen, some as relics kept.
But nevermore the same two sister pearls
Ran down the silken thread to kiss each other
On her white neck—so is it with this rhyme:
It lives dispersedly in many hands,
And every minstrel sings it differently;
Yet is there one true line, the pearl of pearls:
"Man dreams of Fame while woman wakes to love."

96

Yea! Love, though Love were of the grossest, carves
A portion from the solid present, eats
And uses, careless of the rest; but Fame,
The Fame that follows death is nothing to us;
And what is Fame in life but half-disfame,
And counterchanged with darkness? ye yourself
Know well that Envy calls you Devil's son,
And since ye seem the Master of all Art,
They fain would make you Master of all vice.'

And Merlin locked his hand in hers and said,
'I once was looking for a magic weed,
And found a fair young squire who sat alone,
Had carved himself a knightly shield of wood,
And then was painting on it fancied arms,
Azure, an Eagle rising or, the Sun
In dexter chief; the scroll "I follow fame."
And speaking not, but leaning over him
I took his brush and blotted out the bird,
And made a Gardener putting in a graff,
With this for motto, "Rather use than fame."
You should have seen him blush; but afterwards
He made a stalwart knight. O Vivien,
For you, methinks you think you love me well;
For me, I love you somewhat; rest: and Love
Should have some rest and pleasure in himself,
Not ever be too curious for a boon,
Too prurient for a proof against the grain
Of him ye say ye love: but Fame with men,
Being but ampler means to serve mankind,
Should have small rest or pleasure in herself,
But work as vassal to the larger love,
That dwarfs the petty love of one to one.
Use gave me Fame at first, and Fame again
Increasing gave me use. Lo, there my boon!
What other? for men sought to prove me vile,
Because I fain had given them greater wits:
And then did Envy call me Devil's son:
The sick weak beast seeking to help herself
By striking at her better, missed, and brought
Her own claw back, and wounded her own heart.

The Great Book of Merlin

Sweet were the days when I was all unknown,
But when my name was lifted up, the storm
Brake on the mountain and I cared not for it.
Right well know I that Fame is half-disfame,
Yet needs must work my work. That other fame,
To one at least, who hath not children, vague,
The cackle of the unborn about the grave,
I cared not for it: a single misty star,
Which is the second in a line of stars
That seem a sword beneath a belt of three,
I never gazed upon it but I dreamt
Of some vast charm concluded in that star
To make fame nothing. Wherefore, if I fear,
Giving you power upon me through this charm,
That you might play me falsely, having power,
However well ye think ye love me now
(As sons of kings loving in pupilage
Have turned to tyrants when they came to power)
I rather dread the loss of use than fame;
If you—and not so much from wickedness,
As some wild turn of anger, or a mood
Of overstrained affection, it may be,
To keep me all to your own self,—or else
A sudden spurt of woman's jealousy,—
Should try this charm on whom ye say ye love.'

And Vivien answered smiling as in wrath:
'Have I not sworn? I am not trusted. Good!
Well, hide it, hide it; I shall find it out;
And being found take heed of Vivien.
A woman and not trusted, doubtless I
Might feel some sudden turn of anger born
Of your misfaith; and your fine epithet
Is accurate too, for this full love of mine
Without the full heart back may merit well
Your term of overstrained. So used as I,
My daily wonder is, I love at all.
And as to woman's jealousy, O why not?
O to what end, except a jealous one,
And one to make me jealous if I love,
Was this fair charm invented by yourself?

A Book of Merlin

I well believe that all about this world
Ye cage a buxom captive here and there,
Closed in the four walls of a hollow tower
From which is no escape for evermore.'

Then the great Master merrily answered her:
'Full many a love in loving youth was mine;
I needed then no charm to keep them mine
But youth and love; and that full heart of yours
Whereof ye prattle, may now assure you mine;
So live uncharmed. For those who wrought it first,
The wrist is parted from the hand that waved,
The feet unmortised from their ankle-bones
Who paced it, ages back: but will ye hear
The legend as in guerdon for your rhyme?

'There lived a king in the most Eastern East,
Less old than I, yet older, for my blood
Hath earnest in it of far springs to be.
A tawny pirate anchored in his port,
Whose bark had plundered twenty nameless isles;
And passing one, at the high peep of dawn,
He saw two cities in a thousand boats
All fighting for a woman on the sea.
And pushing his black craft among them all,
He lightly scattered theirs and brought her off,
With loss of half his people arrow-slain;
A maid so smooth, so white, so wonderful,
They said a light came from her when she moved:
And since the pirate would not yield her up,
The King impaled him for his piracy;
Then made her Queen: but those isle-nurtured eyes
Waged such unwilling though successful war
On all the youth, they sickened; councils thinned,
And armies waned, for magnet-like she drew
The rustiest iron of old fighters' hearts;
And beasts themselves would worship; camels knelt
Unbidden, and the brutes of mountain back
That carry kings in castles, bowed black knees
Of homage, ringing with their serpent hands,
To make her smile, her golden ankle-bells.

The Great Book of Merlin

What wonder, being jealous, that he sent
His horns of proclamation out through all
The hundred under-kingdoms that he swayed
To find a wizard who might teach the King
Some charm, which being wrought upon the Queen
Might keep her all his own: to such a one
He promised more than ever king has given,
A league of mountain full of golden mines,
A province with a hundred miles of coast,
A palace and a princess, all for him:
But on all those who tried and failed, the King
Pronounced a dismal sentence, meaning by it
To keep the list low and pretenders back,
Or like a king, not to be trifled with—
Their heads should moulder on the city gates.
And many tried and failed, because the charm
Of nature in her overbore their own:
And many a wizard brow bleached on the walls:
And many weeks a troop of carrion crows
Hung like a cloud above the gateway towers.'

And Vivien breaking in upon him, said:
'I sit and gather honey; yet, methinks,
Thy tongue has tript a little: ask thyself.
The lady never made UNWILLING war
With those fine eyes: she had her pleasure in it,
And made her good man jealous with good cause.
And lived there neither dame nor damsel then
Wroth at a lover's loss? were all as tame,
I mean, as noble, as the Queen was fair?
Not one to flirt a venom at her eyes,
Or pinch a murderous dust into her drink,
Or make her paler with a poisoned rose?
Well, those were not our days: but did they find
A wizard? Tell me, was he like to thee?

She ceased, and made her lithe arm round his neck
Tighten, and then drew back, and let her eyes
Speak for her, glowing on him, like a bride's
On her new lord, her own, the first of men.

He answered laughing, 'Nay, not like to me.
At last they found—his foragers for charms—
A little glassy-headed hairless man,
Who lived alone in a great wild on grass;
Read but one book, and ever reading grew
So grated down and filed away with thought,
So lean his eyes were monstrous; while the skin
Clung but to crate and basket, ribs and spine.
And since he kept his mind on one sole aim,
Nor ever touched fierce wine, nor tasted flesh,
Nor owned a sensual wish, to him the wall
That sunders ghosts and shadow-casting men
Became a crystal, and he saw them through it,
And heard their voices talk behind the wall,
And learnt their elemental secrets, powers
And forces; often o'er the sun's bright eye
Drew the vast eyelid of an inky cloud,
And lashed it at the base with slanting storm;
Or in the noon of mist and driving rain,
When the lake whitened and the pinewood roared,
And the cairned mountain was a shadow, sunned
The world to peace again: here was the man.
And so by force they dragged him to the King.
And then he taught the King to charm the Queen
In such-wise, that no man could see her more,
Nor saw she save the King, who wrought the charm,
Coming and going, and she lay as dead,
And lost all use of life: but when the King
Made proffer of the league of golden mines,
The province with a hundred miles of coast,
The palace and the princess, that old man
Went back to his old wild, and lived on grass,
And vanished, and his book came down to me.'

And Vivien answered smiling saucily:
'Ye have the book: the charm is written in it:
Good: take my counsel: let me know it at once:
For keep it like a puzzle chest in chest,
With each chest locked and padlocked thirty-fold,
And whelm all this beneath as vast a mound
As after furious battle turfs the slain

The Great Book of Merlin

On some wild down above the windy deep,
I yet should strike upon a sudden means
To dig, pick, open, find and read the charm:
Then, if I tried it, who should blame me then?'

And smiling as a master smiles at one
That is not of his school, nor any school
But that where blind and naked Ignorance
Delivers brawling judgments, unashamed,
On all things all day long, he answered her:

'Thou read the book, my pretty Vivien!
O ay, it is but twenty pages long,
But every page having an ample marge,
And every marge enclosing in the midst
A square of text that looks a little blot,
The text no larger than the limbs of fleas;
And every square of text an awful charm,
Writ in a language that has long gone by.
So long, that mountains have arisen since
With cities on their flanks—thou read the book!
And ever margin scribbled, crost, and crammed
With comment, densest condensation, hard
To mind and eye; but the long sleepless nights
Of my long life have made it easy to me.
And none can read the text, not even I;
And none can read the comment but myself;
And in the comment did I find the charm.
O, the results are simple; a mere child
Might use it to the harm of anyone,
And never could undo it: ask no more:
For though you should not prove it upon me,
But keep that oath ye sware, ye might, perchance,
Assay it on some one of the Table Round,
And all because ye dream they babble of you.'

And Vivien, frowning in true anger, said:
'What dare the full-fed liars say of me?
THEY ride abroad redressing human wrongs!
They sit with knife in meat and wine in horn!
THEY bound to holy vows of chastity!

A Book of Merlin

Were I not woman, I could tell a tale.
But you are man, you well can understand
The shame that cannot be explained for shame.
Not one of all the drove should touch me: swine!'

Then answered Merlin careless of her words:
'You breathe but accusation vast and vague,
Spleen-born, I think, and proofless. If ye know,
Set up the charge ye know, to stand or fall!'

And Vivien answered frowning wrathfully:
'O ay, what say ye to Sir Valence, him
Whose kinsman left him watcher o'er his wife
And two fair babes, and went to distant lands;
Was one year gone, and on returning found
Not two but three? there lay the reckling, one
But one hour old! What said the happy sire?'
A seven-months' babe had been a truer gift.
Those twelve sweet moons confused his fatherhood.'

Then answered Merlin, 'Nay, I know the tale.
Sir Valence wedded with an outland dame:
Some cause had kept him sundered from his wife:
One child they had: it lived with her: she died:
His kinsman travelling on his own affair
Was charged by Valence to bring home the child.
He brought, not found it therefore: take the truth.'

'O ay,' said Vivien, 'overtrue a tale.
What say ye then to sweet Sir Sagramore,
That ardent man? "to pluck the flower in season,"
So says the song, "I trow it is no treason."
O Master, shall we call him overquick
To crop his own sweet rose before the hour?'

And Merlin answered, 'Overquick art thou
To catch a loathly plume fallen from the wing
Of that foul bird of rapine whose whole prey
Is man's good name: he never wronged his bride.
I know the tale. An angry gust of wind
Puffed out his torch among the myriad-roomed

And many-corridored complexities
Of Arthur's palace: then he found a door,
And darkling felt the sculptured ornament
That wreathen round it made it seem his own;
And wearied out made for the couch and slept,
A stainless man beside a stainless maid;
And either slept, nor knew of other there;
Till the high dawn piercing the royal rose
In Arthur's casement glimmered chastely down,
Blushing upon them blushing, and at once
He rose without a word and parted from her:
But when the thing was blazed about the court,
The brute world howling forced them into bonds,
And as it chanced they are happy, being pure.'

'O ay,' said Vivien, 'that were likely too.
What say ye then to fair Sir Percivale
And of the horrid foulness that he wrought,
The saintly youth, the spotless lamb of Christ,
Or some black wether of St Satan's fold.
What, in the precincts of the chapel-yard,
Among the knightly brasses of the graves,
And by the cold Hic Jacets of the dead!'

And Merlin answered careless of her charge,
'A sober man is Percivale and pure;
But once in life was flustered with new wine,
Then paced for coolness in the chapel-yard;
Where one of Satan's shepherdesses caught
And meant to stamp him with her master's mark;
And that he sinned is not believable;
For, look upon his face!—but if he sinned,
The sin that practice burns into the blood,
And not the one dark hour which brings remorse,
Will brand us, after, of whose fold we be:
Or else were he, the holy king, whose hymns
Are chanted in the minster, worse than all.
But is your spleen frothed out, or have ye more?'

And Vivien answered frowning yet in wrath:
'O ay; what say ye to Sir Lancelot, friend

Traitor or true? that commerce with the Queen,
I ask you, is it clamoured by the child,
Or whispered in the corner? do ye know it?'

To which he answered sadly, 'Yea, I know it.
Sir Lancelot went ambassador, at first,
To fetch her, and she watched him from her walls.
A rumour runs, she took him for the King,
So fixt her fancy on him: let them be.
But have ye no one word of loyal praise
For Arthur, blameless King and stainless man?'

She answered with a low and chuckling laugh:
'Man! is he man at all, who knows and winks?
Sees what his fair bride is and does, and winks?
By which the good King means to blind himself,
And blinds himself and all the Table Round
To all the foulness that they work. Myself
Could call him (were it not for womanhood)
The pretty, popular cause such manhood earns,
Could call him the main cause of all their crime;
Yea, were he not crowned King, coward, and fool.'

Then Merlin to his own heart, loathing, said:
'O true and tender! O my liege and King!
O selfless man and stainless gentleman,
Who wouldst against thine own eye-witness fain
Have all men true and leal, all women pure;
How, in the mouths of base interpreters,
From over-fineness not intelligible
To things with every sense as false and foul
As the poached filth that floods the middle street,
Is thy white blamelessness accounted blame!'

But Vivien, deeming Merlin overborne
By instance, recommenced, and let her tongue
Rage like a fire among the noblest names,
Polluting, and imputing her whole self,
Defaming and defacing, till she left
Not even Lancelot brave, nor Galahad clean.

Her words had issue other than she willed.
He dragged his eyebrow bushes down, and made
A snowy penthouse for his hollow eyes,
And muttered in himself, 'Tell HER the charm!
So, if she had it, would she rail on me
To snare the next, and if she have it not
So will she rail. What did the wanton say?
"Not mount as high;" we scarce can sink as low:
For men at most differ as Heaven and earth,
But women, worst and best, as Heaven and Hell.
I know the Table Round, my friends of old;
All brave, and many generous, and some chaste.
She cloaks the scar of some repulse with lies;
I well believe she tempted them and failed,
Being so bitter: for fine plots may fail,
Though harlots paint their talk as well as face
With colours of the heart that are not theirs.
I will not let her know: nine tithes of times
Face-flatterer and backbiter are the same.
And they, sweet soul, that most impute a crime
Are pronest to it, and impute themselves,
Wanting the mental range; or low desire
Not to feel lowest makes them level all;
Yea, they would pare the mountain to the plain,
To leave an equal baseness; and in this
Are harlots like the crowd, that if they find
Some stain or blemish in a name of note,
Not grieving that their greatest are so small,
Inflate themselves with some insane delight,
And judge all nature from her feet of clay,
Without the will to lift their eyes, and see
Her godlike head crowned with spiritual fire,
And touching other worlds. I am weary of her.'

He spoke in words part heard, in whispers part,
Half-suffocated in the hoary fell
And many-wintered fleece of throat and chin.
But Vivien, gathering somewhat of his mood,
And hearing 'harlot' muttered twice or thrice,
Leapt from her session on his lap, and stood
Stiff as a viper frozen; loathsome sight,

How from the rosy lips of life and love,
Flashed the bare-grinning skeleton of death!
White was her cheek; sharp breaths of anger puffed
Her fairy nostril out; her hand half-clenched
Went faltering sideways downward to her belt,
And feeling; had she found a dagger there
(For in a wink the false love turns to hate)
She would have stabbed him; but she found it not:
His eye was calm, and suddenly she took
To bitter weeping like a beaten child,
A long, long weeping, not consolable.
Then her false voice made way, broken with sobs:

'O crueller than was ever told in tale,
Or sung in song! O vainly lavished love!
O cruel, there was nothing wild or strange,
Or seeming shameful—for what shame in love,
So love be true, and not as yours is—nothing
Poor Vivien had not done to win his trust
Who called her what he called her—all her crime,
All—all—the wish to prove him wholly hers.'

She mused a little, and then clapt her hands
Together with a wailing shriek, and said:
'Stabbed through the heart's affections to the heart!
Seethed like the kid in its own mother's milk!
Killed with a word worse than a life of blows!
I thought that he was gentle, being great:
O God, that I had loved a smaller man!
I should have found in him a greater heart.
O, I, that flattering my true passion, saw
The knights, the court, the King, dark in your light,
Who loved to make men darker than they are,
Because of that high pleasure which I had
To seat you sole upon my pedestal
Of worship—I am answered, and henceforth
The course of life that seemed so flowery to me
With you for guide and master, only you,
Becomes the sea-cliff pathway broken short,
And ending in a ruin—nothing left,
But into some low cave to crawl, and there,

If the wolf spare me, weep my life away,
Killed with inutterable unkindliness.'

She paused, she turned away, she hung her head,
The snake of gold slid from her hair, the braid
Slipt and uncoiled itself, she wept afresh,
And the dark wood grew darker toward the storm
In silence, while his anger slowly died
Within him, till he let his wisdom go
For ease of heart, and half believed her true:
Called her to shelter in the hollow oak,
'Come from the storm,' and having no reply,
Gazed at the heaving shoulder, and the face
Hand-hidden, as for utmost grief or shame;
Then thrice essayed, by tenderest-touching terms,
To sleek her ruffled peace of mind, in vain.
At last she let herself be conquered by him,
And as the cageling newly flown returns,
The seeming-injured simple-hearted thing
Came to her old perch back, and settled there.
There while she sat, half-falling from his knees,
Half-nestled at his heart, and since he saw
The slow tear creep from her closed eyelid yet,
About her, more in kindness than in love,
The gentle wizard cast a shielding arm.
But she dislinked herself at once and rose,
Her arms upon her breast across, and stood,
A virtuous gentlewoman deeply wronged,
Upright and flushed before him: then she said:

'There must now be no passages of love
Betwixt us twain henceforward evermore;
Since, if I be what I am grossly called,
What should be granted which your own gross heart
Would reckon worth the taking? I will go.
In truth, but one thing now—better have died
Thrice than have asked it once—could make me stay—
That proof of trust—so often asked in vain!
How justly, after that vile term of yours,
I find with grief! I might believe you then,
Who knows? once more. Lo! what was once to me

Mere matter of the fancy, now hath grown
The vast necessity of heart and life.
Farewell; think gently of me, for I fear
My fate or folly, passing gayer youth
For one so old, must be to love thee still.
But ere I leave thee let me swear once more
That if I schemed against thy peace in this,
May yon just heaven, that darkens o'er me, send
One flash, that, missing all things else, may make
My scheming brain a cinder, if I lie.'

Scarce had she ceased, when out of heaven a bolt
(For now the storm was close above them) struck,
Furrowing a giant oak, and javelining
With darted spikes and splinters of the wood
The dark earth round. He raised his eyes and saw
The tree that shone white-listed through the gloom.
But Vivien, fearing heaven had heard her oath,
And dazzled by the livid-flickering fork,
And deafened with the stammering cracks and claps
That followed, flying back and crying out,
'O Merlin, though you do not love me, save,
Yet save me!' clung to him and hugged him close;
And called him dear protector in her fright,
Nor yet forgot her practice in her fright,
But wrought upon his mood and hugged him close.
The pale blood of the wizard at her touch
Took gayer colours, like an opal warmed.
She blamed herself for telling hearsay tales:
She shook from fear, and for her fault she wept
Of petulancy; she called him lord and liege,
Her seer, her bard, her silver star of eve,
Her God, her Merlin, the one passionate love
Of her whole life; and ever overhead
Bellowed the tempest, and the rotten branch
Snapt in the rushing of the river-rain
Above them; and in change of glare and gloom
Her eyes and neck glittering went and came;
Till now the storm, its burst of passion spent,
Moaning and calling out of other lands,
Had left the ravaged woodland yet once more

To peace; and what should not have been had been,
For Merlin, overtalked and overworn,
Had yielded, told her all the charm, and slept.

Then, in one moment, she put forth the charm
Of woven paces and of waving hands,
And in the hollow oak he lay as dead,
And lost to life and use and name and fame.

Then crying 'I have made his glory mine,'
And shrieking out 'O fool!' the harlot leapt
Adown the forest, and the thicket closed
Behind her, and the forest echoed 'fool.'

Merlin II

The rhyme of the poet
Modulates the king's affairs;
Balance-loving Nature
Made all things in pairs.
To every foot its antipode;
Each color with its counter glowed;
To every tone beat answering tones,
Higher or graver;
Flavor gladly blends with flavor;
Leaf answers leaf upon the bough;
And match the paired cotyledons.
Hands to hands, and feet to feet,
In one body grooms and brides;
Eldest rite, two married sides
In every mortal meet.
Light's far furnace shines,
Smelting balls and bars,
Forging double stars,
Glittering twins and trines.
The animals are sick with love,
Lovesick with rhyme;
Each with all propitious Time
Into chorus wove.

Like the dancers' ordered band,
Thoughts come also hand in hand;
In equal couples mated,
Or else alternated;
Adding by their mutual gage,
One to other, health and age.
Solitary fancies go
Short-lived wandering to and fro,
Most like to bachelors,
Or an ungiven maid,
Not ancestors,
With no posterity to make the lie afraid,
Or keep truth undecayed.

The Great Book of Merlin

Perfect-paired as eagle's wings,
Justice is the rhyme of things;
Trade and counting use
The self-same tuneful muse;
And Nemesis,
Who with even matches odd,
Who athwart space redresses
The partial wrong,
Fills the just period,
And finishes the song.

Subtle rhymes, with ruin rife,
Murmur in the house of life,
Sung by the Sisters as they spin;
In perfect time and measure they
Build and unbuild our echoing clay,
As the two twilights of the day
Fold us music-drunken in.

Merlin and the Gleam

I.

O YOUNG Mariner,
You from the haven
Under the sea-cliff,
You that are watching
The gray Magician
With eyes of wonder,
I am Merlin,
And I am dying,
I am Merlin
Who follow The Gleam.

II.

Mighty the Wizard
Who found me at sunrise
Sleeping, and woke me
And learn'd me Magic!
Great the Master,
And sweet the Magic,
When over the valley,
In early summers,
Over the mountain,
On human faces,
And all around me,
Moving to melody,
Floated The Gleam.

III.

Once at the croak of a Raven who crost it,
A barbarous people,
Blind to the magic,
And deaf to the melody,

Snarl'd at and cursed me.
A demon vext me,
The light retreated,
The landskip darken'd,
The melody deaden'd,
The Master whisper'd
"Follow The Gleam."

IV.

Then to the melody,
Over a wilderness
Gliding, and glancing at
Elf of the woodland,
Gnome of the cavern,
Griffin and Giant,
And dancing of Fairies
In desolate hollows,
And wraiths of the mountain,
And rolling of dragons
By warble of water,
Or cataract music
Of falling torrents,
Flitted The Gleam.

V.

Down from the mountain
And over the level,
And streaming and shining on
Silent river,
Silvery willow,
Pasture and plowland,
Horses and oxen,
Innocent maidens,
Garrulous children,

Homestead and harvest,
Reaper and gleaner,
And rough-ruddy faces
Of lowly labour,
Slided The Gleam.—

VI.

Then, with a melody
Stronger and statelier,
Led me at length
To the city and palace
Of Arthur the king;
Touch'd at the golden
Cross of the churches,
Flash'd on the Tournament,
Flicker'd and bicker'd
From helmet to helmet,
And last on the forehead
Of Arthur the blameless
Rested The Gleam.

VII.

Clouds and darkness
Closed upon Camelot;
Arthur had vanish'd
I knew not whither,
The king who loved me,
And cannot die;
For out of the darkness
Silent and slowly
The Gleam, that had waned to a wintry glimmer
On icy fallow
And faded forest,
Drew to the valley

Named of the shadow,
And slowly brightening
Out of the glimmer,
And slowly moving again to a melody
Yearningly tender,
Fell on the shadow,
No longer a shadow,
But clothed with The Gleam.

VIII.

And broader and brighter
The Gleam flying onward,
Wed to the melody,
Sang thro' the world;
And slower and fainter,
Old and weary,
But eager to follow,
I saw, whenever
In passing it glanced upon
Hamlet or city,
That under the Crosses
The dead man's garden,
The mortal hillock,
Would break into blossom;
And so to the land's
Last limit I came—
And can no longer,
But die rejoicing,
For thro' the Magic
Of Him the Mighty,
Who taught me in childhood,
There on the border
Of boundless Ocean,
And all but in Heaven
Hovers The Gleam.

IX.

Not of the sunlight,
Not of the moonlight,
Not of the starlight!
O young Mariner,
Down to the haven,
Call your companions,
Launch your vessel,
And crowd your canvas,
And, ere it vanishes
Over the margin,
After it, follow it,
Follow The Gleam.

Excalibur

Right so the king and he departed, and went unto an hermit that was a good man and a great leech. So the hermit searched all his wounds and gave him good salves; so the king was there three days, and then were his wounds well amended that he might ride and go, and so departed. And as they rode, Arthur said, I have no sword. No force, said Merlin, hereby is a sword that shall be yours, an I may. So they rode till they came to a lake, the which was a fair water and broad, and in the midst of the lake Arthur was ware of an arm clothed in white samite, that held a fair sword in that hand. Lo! said Merlin, yonder is that sword that I spake of. With that they saw a damosel going upon the lake. What damosel is that? said Arthur. That is the Lady of the Lake, said Merlin; and within that lake is a rock, and therein is as fair a place as any on earth, and richly beseen; and this damosel will come to you anon, and then speak ye fair to her that she will give you that sword. Anon withal came the damosel unto Arthur, and saluted him, and he her again. Damosel, said Arthur, what sword is that, that yonder the arm holdeth above the water? I would it were mine, for I have no sword. Sir Arthur, king, said the damosel, that sword is mine, and if ye will give me a gift when I ask it you, ye shall have it. By my faith, said Arthur, I will give you what gift ye will ask. Well! said the damosel, go ye into yonder barge, and row yourself to the sword, and take it and the scabbard with you, and I will ask my gift when I see my time. So Sir Arthur and Merlin alighted and tied their horses to two trees, and so they went into the ship, and when they came to the sword that the hand held, Sir Arthur took it up by the handles, and took it with him, and the arm and the hand went under the water. And so [they] came unto the land and rode forth, and then Sir Arthur saw a rich pavilion. What signifieth yonder pavilion? It is the knight's pavilion, said Merlin, that ye fought with last, Sir Pellinore; but he is out, he is not there. He hath ado with a knight of yours that hight Egglame, and they have foughten together, but at the last Egglame fled, and else he had been dead, and he hath chased him even to Carlion, and we shall meet with him anon in the highway. That is well said, said Arthur, now have I a sword, now will I wage battle with him, and be avenged on him. Sir, you shall not so, said Merlin, for the knight is weary of fighting and chasing, so that ye shall have no worship to have ado with him; also he will not be lightly matched of one knight living, and therefore it is my counsel, let him pass, for he shall do you good service in short time, and his sons after his days. Also ye shall see that day in short space, you shall be right glad to give him your sister to wed. When I see him, I will do as ye advise, said Arthur.

Then Sir Arthur looked on the sword, and liked it passing well. Whether liketh you better, said Merlin, the sword or the scabbard? Me liketh better the sword, said Arthur. Ye are more unwise, said Merlin, for the scabbard is worth ten of the swords, for whiles ye have the scabbard upon you, ye shall never lose no blood, be ye never so sore wounded; therefore keep well the scabbard always with you. So they rode unto Carlion, and by the way they met with Sir Pellinore; but Merlin had done such a craft, that Pellinore saw not Arthur, and he passed by without any words. I marvel, said Arthur, that the knight would not speak. Sir, said Merlin, he saw you not, for an he had seen you, ye had not lightly departed. So they came unto Carlion, whereof his knights were passing glad. And when they heard of his adventures, they marvelled that he would jeopard his person so, alone. But all men of worship said it was merry to be under such a chieftain, that would put his person in adventure as other poor knights did.

Merlin's Song

Of Merlin wise I learned a song, –
Sing it low, or sing it loud,
It is mightier than the strong,
And punishes the proud.
I sing it to the surging crowd,—
Good men it will calm and cheer,
Bad men it will chain and cage.
In the heart of the music peals a strain
Which only angels hear;
Whether it waken joy or rage,
Hushed myriads hark in vain,
Yet they who hear it shed their age,
And take their youth again.

Merlin's Grave

Mighty wizard was old Merlin, the wisest of his age;
But Love all living men subdues, and Love spared not the sage:
So the gray-beard grew a dotard for one fair woman's sake,
Ever following and wooing the Ladye of the Lake;
For she chain'd him with her beauty, and ruled him with a smile,
Till he taught her each enchantment, each magic charm and wile;
And on the four Evangelists an oath she made him swear
That his subtle craft should never her life with mysteries snare.

But she loved no whit the wizard: yet, to learn his mystic art,
She feign'd a loving passion, and acted well her part;
And he taught her all the wonders of the fire, earth, and sea,
All the marvels of the genii, all tricks of glamourie,
Gave her words of spell and power the spirits to command,
And gifted her with prophecy, with lore from every land.
But she wearied of the master when his parables were o'er,
And ladies laugh at lovers gray-bearded and three-score.

Thus it happen'd, as they journey'd, he show'd her by the way,
Mid a rock, a deep-hewn cavern, wherein a wonder lay,
But that hitherto was hidden beneath a weighty stone
From the entrance could be shaken by sorcery alone;
Then she pray'd the old magician, with many a witching word,
To venture in and record bear what sights were there interr'd;
In an evil hour Merlin he did the Ladye's will,
For she quickly wrought her magic, and the rock entombs him still.

Long in court and council-chamber they waited for the sage,
And marvell'd what endeavor his absence should engage;
'Twas whisper'd he had wander'd afar beyond the main
To countries of the Orient, and yet would come again,
With more than mortal wisdom, to work for England's weal,
From the sepulchre of Solomon bearing home the sacred seal.
But forever kept the Ladye the secret of the stone,
As she sat beneath the waters and wrought her spells alone.

Merlin's Last Prophecy

"Come ye from far, wild Ocean Daughters!
Shell-borne on the dangerous sea,
With pearly oars that ply the waters,
Say, bright Strangers, whence ye be?"

From a far Isle in unknown waters
Fleeting like mist the windswept sea,
We come—wise Merlin's potent Daughters,
Morgain-le-fay's handmaidens we!

Wide our gossamer sails unfurling,
With coral prow we stem the spray,
Our crisp shell behind us curling
Keeps the plashy surge away.

Fear not baleful charms or chidings,
Sweet our words as dropping balm,
Peace we bring and gentle tidings,
Keep thy heart in holiest calm.

The wild winds lull to our harps' soft numbers,
Lo! when music meet our hands,
Even the restless Ocean slumbers
Hugely on his bed of sands.

Lo! how swift our notes of pleasure
Sparkle along the golden strings,
While in rapturous mood and measure
Her dulcet verse each Maiden sings.

We o'er your land, like Guardian Spirits,
From our far isle of Avalon,
Watch, and o'er all that here inherits,
Beautiful daughter and brave son.

Favour to One grew strong and stronger,
Who from her bright looks aye hath been

A Book of Merlin

Our Princess Fair-star: now no longer,
But Britain's fair and starry Queen.

Say to that young and sovran Beauty
This message hymned to thee alone,
Offering these gifts with proudest duty
At the bright foot which gems her throne.

Morgain to Britain's Queen commendeth
This magic Trident, virtue-stored;
Pendragon's Son, fair greeting, sendeth
Caliburn, his enchanted sword.

Rapt Merlin sings: "where a strengthless Woman
This sceptre holds with a firm strain,
That Land, maugre East and Western foeman,
Shall rule both East and Western main.

Where, with the same small clasp and slender,
This sword pale Resolution draws,
That Land need pray nought else defend her
But grace of God and her good Cause!"

Farewell!—the mortal arms that kept her
Safe, thro' the Past, its rage might quell,
But 'tis no common sword and sceptre
Shall sway Futurity!—Farewell!

Merlín in Avalon

How good Sir Cephalus did save
Merlin from subterranean grave
Who bids him fly on speedy wing
And with an apple wake the King
While Merlin hasteneth to make fall
By magic art the lodestone wall.

WHEN Sir Cephalus heard these words he was mightily perplexed, and
he said: "Who are these that sing, and what is it that they say? They seem
to be men coming in haste out of Britain, and to think that King Arthur
is about to return to their land; but of the words that they use I can make
nothing; nor can I think what is a 'debenture,' or a 'speculation,' or a
'syndicate' or a 'corner,' since these are words that were not used in Britain
in King Arthur's time: I cannot tell what they say. Nevertheless, they have
put a good thought into my mind. For I mind well that in Britain Merlin
was wont to prophesy that King Arthur would pass much time in the Island
of Avalon, and should be healed there of his wounds; but that afterwards
he should come again into Britain, and it may be that this prophecy is
about to be accomplished. Therefore it is most surely expedient that, if it
be possible, I should wake the King; but how this is to be done, and, when
it is done, what is to be done next, is more than I can tell." Once again
therefore he fell into deep sorrow and dismay; but, as he pondered in his
heart, he heard close by him, but under the earth, a deep groan, and,
paying heed thereto, he was aware of a voice proceeding out of a cave, and
crying to him: "Sir Cephalus! Sir Cephalus! Sir Cephalus!" "Who art
thou," said Sir Cephalus, "who callest upon me?" "I am Merlin," said the
voice, "which was buried alive; and I am in great pain, because I have
made a prophecy; and I have heard voices of the Bulls and the Bears
whereby I wot well the time has come when the prophecy should be
accomplished; yet cannot I accomplish it, because I am in prison, and have
no man to set me free: but were I loose, know of a surety that I could
deliver thee and thy fellows from Morgan la Faye, and bring to nought her
foul enchantments." "What must I do," said Sir Cephalus, "to set thee
free?" "Thou must, first of all," said the voice, "lay a stick upon the
ground, and leap over it backwards three times; then strew vervain and dill
upon the mouth of the cave, and cry with a loud voice, 'Aum mani
padméhoum, and, when all this has been done, the stone whereunder I am

bound will be rolled away, and I shall be able to come forth to the upper air, after which I will tell thee what more thou must do." In all these things Sir Cephalus did what the voice bade him; and forwithal there came from the cave with pain and difficulty an ancient man, whose beard had grown so long that it had wound all round him, as ivy about an oak, and had wrapped his limbs as it were with a cere-cloth. But when he came into the light and air he seemed to renew his manhood and vigour, and anon he appeared to Sir Cephalus in that disguise wherein he had formerly appeared to King Arthur, namely, all furred with black sheep-skins and with a great pair of boots and a russet gown, and with wild geese in his hand: whereby Sir Cephalus knew of a surety that it was Merlin, and he rejoiced greatly to see him again. "Truly," said Merlin, "the light is good, and a pleasant thing it is for the eyes to behold the sun; but now let me deliver to thee the prophecy for the accomplishment whereof I am in labour, which indeed I made of old in Latin." Right so he lifted up his voice in a loud chant to this purpose, for so what he said may be rendered in the British tongue:

"After this shall the red dragon return to his own manners, and turn his rage upon himself. A blessed King shall prepare a fleet, and shall be reckoned the twelfth in the Court of Saints. There shall be a miserable desolation of the kingdom and the threshing-floors of the harvests shall return to unfruitful forests. The white dragon shall rise again, and invite over a daughter of Germany. Our gardens shall be again replenished with foreign seed, and the red dragon shall pine away at the end of the marsh. After that shall the German worm be crowned, and the brazen prince buried. He has his bounds assigned him which he shall not be able to fly over."

"Now, Sir Cephalus," said Merlin, "what dost thou think of this ancient prophecy?" "Truly," said Sir Cephalus, "I think that thou art talking gibberish." "That may well be," said Merlin; "nevertheless, these things are in a fair way to be accomplished. But now listen to my words. Thou must go, first of all, to the Lutons, and bid them take off their crowns of forgetfulness, that they may see clearly the case wherein they be, and then they also will desire, as thou dost, to wake King Arthur. Then go all together to rouse the King out of his sleep, and for this purpose place against his lips one of the Apples of Ennui, and when he is awake pray him to take off his head the crown of forgetfulness. After that ye shall all return to me, and, I will show you what things I will do to Morgan la Faye and her kingdom."

Right so sped away Sir Cephalus, and coming to the Lutons, he cried: "Worthy Lutons, take the crowns from off your heads, and see clearly the case wherein we all be; for Merlin has come to life, and hath uttered to me what soundeth like gibberish, but as he tells me, is a prophecy like to be accomplished." Whereupon the Lutons did as Sir Cephalus bade them; and when they had taken off their crowns their memories came back to them, and they saw that they were not truly in Britain, but that all around them the high wall of lodestone shut them off from the world without. Whereat they were horribly dismayed; but Sir Cephalus told them that if they waked King Arthur, all would be well, since Merlin knew what things ought afterwards to be done. They came therefore to the king, and found him asleep; but when Sir Cephalus touched his lips with the Apple of Ennui, he woke with a start and yawned mightily. And at first he knew not where he was, but when Sir Cephalus prayed him to remove his crown, he saw, like the rest, that he was in a great dungeon; and he called with a dreadful voice to bring him his sword Excalibur, that with it he might hew in pieces Morgan la Faye. So they brought Excalibur to him; but before he set forth to find the Queen there was a mighty sound, as of thunder, and a great earthquake, after which King Arthur and they that were with him looked abroad, and saw that the wall of lodestone was no longer standing; but they could see far away over the seas towards Britain; and they saw Merlin standing on a rock with his wizard's wand, and gathered all round the island was a multitude of folk such as no man could number, shouting aloud, and asking that Arthur their King might be brought forth to them.

What Merlin did doth Geoffrey say
To Table Round and Morgan Faye.

WHEN Sir Cephalus and the company of the Round Table came where Merlin was, Merlin said unto them: "Worthy knights, we have many things yet to perform, and the first of them is to make a fell arrest of Morgan la Faye, who hath wrought all these enchantments in Avalon, and now shall ye mark well the judgment that shall fall upon her." So he bade Morgan come forth in her true shape; and she, who was wont to appear before the eyes of the Round Table in all the marvel of her beauty, was now seen to be even as her sister Alcina, when she was transformed to her true shape by the fairy Logistilla, of whom the history saith: "Alcina's face was pale, wrinkled, and lean; her stature shrank to less than six spans; every tooth had fallen out of her mouth: for she had lived longer than Hecuba and the Cumæan Sibyl, and indeed than any other woman, but she made such use of arts unknown to our time that she could appear ever beautiful and young." And when they saw Morgan as she really was, all the men of Avalon loathed her.

After this Merlin said unto King Arthur: "Now will I join again the Round Table which Morgan cut in half; and there shall be no more a division between them that sit at the high dais and them that sit at the lower end of the Hall; but all shall dine together at the Round Table, as in the days when King Leodegrance gave it thee as a gift. Nor shall they play any longer at the game of Loaves and Fishes, or observe the rule of Let Be; but thou thyself shalt choose whom thou wilt to be thy ministers, even those whom the people shall judge to be the hablest to give thee counsel in defence of thy Empire." This therefore Merlin did, and he joined together the Round Table, making for it one hundred and fifty sieges, as in the days of old, for those who should be judged worthy to dine with the King. But King Arthur said to him: "Now, Merlin, hast thou done all these things marvellously; yet it appears not what I must do to recover my kingdom. To Britain we must surely return; but I see well that the Island of Britain is filled full of folk of whom I know nothing; nor do I know what things have passed in Britain since the days when Morgan led me away to Avalon, so that I shall not be able to rule my people with wisdom and judgment."

Merlin of astral bodies' state
Doth many marvels here relate
And how by his almighty spells
It came to pass, as Geoffrey tells
That all the elves at his command
Returned once more from Fairyland
How beneath the waves these elves
So wondrously bestirred themselves
That from sea-bottom they did raise
The vanished world of ancient days
When Arthur might new realms possess
And reign in land of Lyonnesse.

The Great Book of Merlin

MERLIN answered: "My liege lord, it is indeed not fitting that thou shouldest return to Britain knowing nothing of the things that have happened since thy passing away; nor will the records of those things that passed before the days of Uther Pendragon help thee altogether to govern aright; but for this there is a remedy. Well, I wot, thou rememberest that ancient land of Lyonnesse in Cornwall, where thou was wont sometime to take thy pleasure, and where Sir Tristram made his book of Venerie, and where Sir Palamedes all his lifetime followed the Questing Beast. This land, after thy passing into Avalon, was, as all good historians tell, by magic art sundered from the mainland, and sunk beneath the sea with one hundred and forty churches, and there it lies to this day. Moreover, it is known unto me that the memories of all things that have happened in Britain, when they are once past and gone, sink down into Lyonnesse and are preserved there for ever; and true copies of those past things remain in Lyonnesse, even as Morgan la Faye was able by her arts to preserve in this Island of Avalon false copies of those things which thou thyself didst remember in Britain." "How shall that avail me?" said King Arthur, "seeing that Lyonnesse is at the bottom of the sea; and I love not to rule there any better than in Avalon?" "We will," said Merlin, "certainly have it up, and thou shalt reign there, and all the Britons shall acknowledge thee for their lord and Emperor." "How may that be?" said the King. "I will tell you," said Merlin. "Be it known unto you all that, though my corporeal body was, by Morgan's arts, confined in Avalon these many hundreds of years, my astral body was free to move over the earth; and by keeping company with other men's souls, I have learned more of the magic art than ever I knew when thou, my liege, wast King in Britain. For in these ages I became acquainted with the magician Paracelsus, and with his disciples, Dee and Kelly; and these discovered to me many secrets; but far more have I learned from the great Fay Blavatsky, who was versed in all the mystic lore of the ancient Egyptians, and who unveiled to me the secret of Isis. She taught me many spells, and with one of these I will summon all the elves to come again from Fairyland, whither they long ago retired after I ceased to make use of them; and I will bid them lift Lyonnesse, with all that is therein, from the bottom of the sea." " Now, by my troth," said King Arthur, "I ever knew thee to be a good magician; but if thou canst do as thou sayest, I will maintain on my body that no conjurer can hold a candle to thee." So Merlin stood upon the rock where he was, and cried with a loud voice:—

"Abracadabra!
I conjure you,
Come into view,
Spirits that do, and do, and do!
Come by your troth
To the name of Thoth,
By Solomon's Seal; by the Mason's Oath;
By the mystic Serpent that bites his tail;
By the Nose of Isis behind her veil;
By the holy Elixir, each drop and each dreg;
By the yolk of the Philosophical Egg;
By Squares and by Curves;
By each drug that serves
To excite the highly fatidical nerves,
Or to slip the soul from its fleshly leash,
Opium, Soma, sweet Hascheesch;
By Female and Male; by False and by True;
By White wine and Red; by Black eye and Blue;
By Odd and by Even;
By Five and by Seven;
And by everything else 'twixt the earth and the heaven;
Spirits that do, and do, and do!
Come into view,
I conjure you!
Abracadabra!"

Right marvellous was it to hear, after Merlin had uttered this spell, how he was answered by many voices, which seemed to come from over the seas; and this is what they sang:—

"Fays and elves, there was a time,
"In the young world's wondering prime,
"When through earth, and air, and sea,
"Joyous in each untravelled zone,
Imperial Fancy wandered fair and free,
And made the realms of Science all her own.
Oft in the alembic of the mind,
She, like an alchemist, refined,

And blending all that Eld or Thought
Of strange, and rare, and fearful found,
From the mixed elements she wrought—
Featly wrought and made appear—
A bright and magic atmosphere,
Within whose pure ethereal bound,
The race of her attendant elves
Might viewlessly disport themselves,
And ere the dawn, in crystal dew-drop clear,
Or in the colours of the evening sky,
Might pour rare music on the enchanted ear,
And raise sweet visions for the illumined eye.

"Mountain, moor, and meadow then,
And the roofs of mortal men,
In the moonlight hours were free
To the fairies' revelry;
Save where the horse-shoe's warning glint
Forbade the way, or hollow flint,
Hung nightly by the manger's stook:
Then would they meet by running brook;
And often in the ingle's glow
The elfin dancers to and fro
Upon the sanded floor were seen,
In scarlet cap and kirtle green,
Scarce than man's middle finger higher,
While winked and fell the midnight fire:
And oft they slid on pale moonbeam
Into the thrifty scullion's dream,
Or to the hind on mountain road,
Upon the Baptist's Vigil, showed,
Far glimmering through the twilight air,
The Commerce of the Pixy Fair,
Them too the early shepherd in the Down,
Driving his flock to pasture, sometimes spied,
While yet they danced their circle on the crown,
Or trod the wild-thyme by the borstal's side;
There might he see them halt to hark

The first light matins of the lark,
Or the faint stir within the waking farm;
Might watch them shiver at the house-dog's bark,
And, when the glimmering east was gray,
Break off their uncompleted charm,
And with the first shrill cock-crow fade away.

"Then, Elves and Fairies, came a time,
In the late world's perished prime,
When in that magic atmosphere
The orb of Fancy seemed to wane,
And Science dared behind the veil to peer,
And search the holy ground with eye profane;
And, breaking on those realms of Eld,
By fair Imagination held,
Austere Experience, with his judging brain,
The bright illusions of the earth dispelled.
Then all the race of fay and sprite
Dwindled in the dryer light;
And, vanishing in upper air,
The radiant vapour heavenward rolled,
And left in roofless ruin bare
The temples, where ancestral lore
Had fixed their habitations old,
Primeval caves of bedded ore,
And mystic stones by stream and wold.
Then from their violated haunts
Forth passed the Fairy emigrants,
And some were seen to ride, a shadowy band,
With steadfast faces set to western shore,
Whence o'er the waves they passed to Fairyland,
And in the mortal world appeared no more.

"But lo! how Magic lifts her head,
And bids the old illusion spread!
The elves from Fairyland return:
For Britain's shores their spirits yearn.
Say, Merlin, say (for thou dost know)

The Great Book of Merlin

What scenes of pleasure, long ago
Remembered, still shall yield delight
To us, gay wanderers of the night:
Whether on high South Saxon hill,
We shall afar distinguish still
The sails of some late-grinding mill,
Winnowing the darkness; or admire,
Poised on the point of shingled spire,
The red-tiled village sound asleep;
Or through the perilous key-hole creep
To seek the cream-bowl, or renew
The silver penny in the shoe;
Or hark for sound of holy spring
To dip our latest changëling.
Or shall we scent 'mid oaken copse
Perfumes of the drying hops,
Where curls the smoke from the cowl'd oast.
And round and round, like fleeting ghost,
The owlet hears in moonlight pale
Sound through the barn the fairy flail?
Or, speeding southwards, shall we spy
The long soft line against the sky,
As the shadowy Downs draw nigh,
Above all places to the Fairies sweet?
Nowhere is the circling air,
Half so delicate and rare,
No turf so nimble to the dancers' feet!
There from the gorse how sudden spring
Wheat-ear and whin-chat on the wing!
And there is many a magic flower,
The crow's-foot and the pimpernel,
Proper for Oberon's throne, Titania's bower;
And greener circles fit for potent spell,
When after elfin wassail, fleet and merry,
We trip beneath thy towers, grey Arundel,
Or haunt thy moon-lit Ring, sweet Chanctonbury."

Now by this time the whole shore was covered with the armies of the elves, and Merlin said to them: "Be not idle! I did not call ye to sing, but to labour; albeit song is not forbidden to ye, if ye perform your task, for as the poet saith, 'Verse soothes the soul, however rude the sound.' But what ye have to do before sunset is to lift the land of Lyonnesse from the bottom of the sea; and when ye have done this, ye have freedom to go where ye will, even as ye did of old in the land of Britain." Then all the elves with one accord passed under the sea and laboured mightily, and presently their voices were heard coming upwards from the deep, so that all men might listen to their song:—

"Where lies the strand of the buried land?
Beneath thy cliffs, Bottreaux,
The voice of thy bells or sinks or swells
Before the storm-winds blow,
And Tresco's wave roofs in the grave
Where the Admiral lies full low.
About his head, in a tomb's stead,
The bars of the earth stand fast;
Around his feet no winding sheet,
But anchor, and weed, and mast,
And whatever of old the waves have rolled
From the wrecks of ages past.
All round it range wide ruin and change,
But, firm in that sunken shore,
Stands ever in sight the Image bright
Of the Vanished Days of Yore.

"Then with swift toil from the sea-weed's coil
A thousand cables weave:
Your levers thrust 'neath the ocean's crust,
And the axe and the crowbar heave!
Haste, haste! there fall on the waving wall
The paling lights of eve!
Heave ho! heave ho! The roots below
Are wrenching with the strain;
Earth's fibres part: the rock-bars start;
Again! again! again!
Aid, Merlin, aid! the mass, up-weighed,

Is mounting through the main:
And now it rides on the buoyant tides,
And greets the sun once more;
And, as long ago, the last beams glow
On the Risen Days of Yore.

"From the deep sea springs long vanished things
On the earth's glad face are seen:
How fresh and fair is the wave-washed air!
And the rivers are bright and clean:
And the sound is blithe of the sharpened scythe
On the uplands waving green:
And the evening flail rings down the vale,
While the reapers through the land
Heave high the shock in ribbon and smock,
Well broidered by the hand:
And they dance and they dine 'neath the Tabard's sign
And the Maypole from the Strand.
Look up and down you see no town,
With its smoke, and money, and roar;
But meadow and wood, as Britain stood,
In the Country Days of Yore.

"From the waves afar the Calendar
Comes free from blur and taint;
And the bells have chimes of the Catholic times,
To keep the folk acquaint
With the holy tides, as the year divides,
And the day's appointed Saint.
The lowly and great they mark the date
By the rosemary and the bays,
And the offered mite for the Plough-Light,
And the wool of good St Blase,
And the ale and the cakes of a hundred wakes,
And the flowers of the old May Days;
When the psalms of the bird ofttimes were heard
From his hawthorn church to pour,
And each bough above sang praise to Love

A Book of Merlin

On the Festal Days of Yore.

"No brow looks sour in the evening hour,
For labour here is free;
And each may hold for his service told
His fruitful plot in fee,
When they love to foil black Care and Toil
With mirth and minstrelsie.
They fill the horn to John Barleycorn,
When first they plough the loam,
And make good cheer when the sheep they shear
And card the wool, or comb,
And with carol and lay, they cart the hay,
Or bring the harvest home.
And the goodwife's zeal spins round the wheel
Beside the cottage door,
As in circling track Time's course brings back
The Mirthful Days of Yore.

"From the dreadful gulf that roars round Wolf,
And his beacon blazing red,
Let the tidings wend to wild Land's End,
Or high Rosemullion Head,
And north to Bude, through the solitude
Of old Dundagel, spread!
On granite and bluff this eve the chough
Unmarked shall ply the wing,
While the fishermen wait if the sea-wind late
May the blare of a trumpet bring,
Or watch on the marge for a coming barge
To waft them back their King.
To each sight and sound their hearts rebound,
As dream and hope restore,
In Faery light the Image bright
Of the Knightly Days of Yore."

Merlin's Tomb

PART FIRST.

Ah fatal thirst — Ah fond aspire
    Forbidden things to know!
Dis-Edener thou of our first sire!
    Well-spring of all our woe!

The first device the tempter tried,
    Thou art his favourite still,
Dost woo and win him, his witch-bride,
    Soul-pledged to work his will.

****

King Arthur weeps in Carduel,
    His Merlin's mystic doom —
Sir Gawayne rides o'er down and dell
    In search of Merlin's tomb.

But vain the quest. Betrayed by thee,
    With sinful love to aid,
In airy tower that none may see
    Is mighty Merlin laid.

****

"Sir Merlin, thou hast taught me long,
    And taught me wondrous well,
The magic power of sign and song,
    And necromantic spell."

(Thus spake the Lady Viviane,
    It is peerless paramoure,
As they in dalliance fond and fain
    Lay in their forest bower.)

"And I can bid the bright noontide

A Book of Merlin

Turn to a midnight gloom,
And toothless crone seem bonny bride
To mock the gay bridegroom.

"And I can tame the proudest knight,
And change to hart or hare,
And crowd with keep and castled height
The void abyme of air.

"And I can bridge the ocean-stream;
On moorland waste and wild,
Bid forest wave, or palace gleam
By silver lake in-isled.

"And I can wake ærial strain,
The moping mood to cheer,
As viol, lute, orpherien,
Did mix sweet music near.

"And I can bid with hound and horn
The mimic huntsman ride
With shout o'er fell and forest borne,
Athwart the welkin wide.

"And I can make knight, countering knight,
Career with levelled lance,
Or dames and squires to bevy bright
In masque or merry dance.

"But there's one thing I cannot do;
I pray thee teach it me —"
(And round his neck her arms she threw,
And kissed him coaxingly.)

"How might a lady have her still
Her lord in loving bower,
Whence he could not, save at her will,
Without or wall or tower?

The Great Book of Merlin

"Can magic build me bower like this?
    O sweet methinks it were
In such a bower in life-long bliss
    To hold thee prisoner!

"A happy bondman shouldst thou be —
    A gentle jailer I —
When thou would'st forth, mine only fee
    A kiss — thy ransom high."

Sir Merlin frowned — Sir Merlin sighed,
    But as entranced he lay
On that fair breast, his purpose died,
    He could not say her nay.

Ne'er loved the Lady Viviane,
    It seemed so fondly well,
And long I ween ere morning dawn,
    She learned that fatal spell!

PART SECOND.

In May, when flowers are springing fair,
    And woods are bourgeoning,
And lustly love in earth and air
    Lordeth each living thing,

Sir Merlin and his peerless make
    Are wandering hand in hand
By flowery dell and forest brake
    Through fair Broceliande

They drank them of that magic fount
    Renowned in minstrel song,
That gusheth from his stony mount —
    Enchanted Berenton!

As by the wizard well they stood

— To prove the legend true —
Against the rock in sportive mood
    Some sprinkled drops they threw.

Amain, aloud, from shivered cloud
    It dashed the drenching shower,
Beneath a linden's leafy shroud
    The laughing lovers cower.

Then gaily on their way they wend
    Thorough that forest fair,
In ferny glade, and briery bend,
    Startling the hind and hare.

With linked arm in amorous talk
    They stroll the forest through,
And clasp and kiss in lone wood-walk,
    As loving pair will do.

Anon they reached the fairest nook
    In that fair wood, a bower
O'er which a hoary hawthorn shook
    Odorous its blossoms' shower.

The spot was fair, the lovers fain;
    Beneath that hawthorn tree
Sir Merlin and fair Viviane
    Disport them lovingly.

****

But summer's ray, and lover's play,
    Will medicine kindly sleep;
On Viviane's lap Sir Merlin lay
    And sunk in slumber deep.

The lady looked — "He slumbers well,"
    (She thought — ah wo the hour!)

The Great Book of Merlin

"Now is the time to prove my spell —
    My spell of wondrous power!"

Gently Sir Merlin's head she's placed,
    And slowly, on the ground;
Then muttering, with her wimple traced
    A ring the hawthorn round.

Nine times that magic ring she made —
    Nine times that spell she spoke,
Then on her lap the slumberer laid;
    But when Sir Merlin woke,

He looked a wild, he looked a long
    Upon his prison-bower;
It seemed a castle fair and strong,
    Begirt with trench and tower.

Sir Merlin frown'd, Sir Merlin sigh'd,
    Fair Viviane laughed the while;
"Such fortune still must fool betide
    Will trust a woman's wile!

"The fatal coil thine art hath wove
    Thine art can ne'er undo!"
And long with mightiest spell she strove,
    But ah! she found it true.

And there that lady fond and fair —
    The Lady of the Lake —
By day, by night, will oft repair
    Her sweet solace to take.

But Arthur weeps in Carduel
    His Merlin's mystic doom;
And Gawayne seeks, by down and dell,
    In vain for Merlin's tomb!